Readers love
KC Burn

Tea or Consequences

"It thrilled my mystery-loving heart. If you enjoy a mystery and a yummy romance, this one might be your cuppa… (tea, that is.)"

—Joyfully Jay

"If you want a book that will captivate you and have you thinking the whole way through, then this book is right up your street, it's a perfect little whodunnit."

—OptimuMM

Just Add Argyle

"I can't recommend *Just Add Argyle* enough!! The story is intense, the depth of emotion behind the writing is just, WOW!"

—Love Bytes

"This was an amazing read and definitely on my recommended list."

—Gay Book Reviews

Plaid versus Paisley

"KC Burns gave us two lovable characters with flaws and struggles that not only endeared me to them but I cheered for on the sidelines."

—Diverse Reader

"*Plaid versus Paisley* proved to be a satisfying, worthwhile read…"

—Just Love: Queer Book Reviews

By KC BURN

Banded Together
Grand Adventures (Dreamspinner Anthology)
One Pulse (Dreamspinner Anthology)
Pen Name – Doctor Chicken
Rainbow Blues
Tea or Consequences

FABRIC HEARTS
Tartan Candy
Plaid versus Paisley
Just Add Argyle

TORONTO TALES
Cop Out
Cover Up
Cast Off

Published by DREAMSPINNER PRESS
www.dreamspinnerpress.com

BANDED TOGETHER

KC BURN

Published by
DREAMSPINNER PRESS

5032 Capital Circle SW, Suite 2, PMB# 279, Tallahassee, FL 32305-7886 USA
www.dreamspinnerpress.com

This is a work of fiction. Names, characters, places, and incidents either are the product of author imagination or are used fictitiously, and any resemblance to actual persons, living or dead, business establishments, events, or locales is entirely coincidental.

ISBN: 978-1-64080-147-9
Digital ISBN: 978-1-64080-148-6
Library of Congress Control Number: 2017911494
Published December 2017
v. 1.0

Printed in the United States of America
∞
This paper meets the requirements of
ANSI/NISO Z39.48-1992 (Permanence of Paper).

To the bands of my misspent youth and a few newer loves:

Skinny Puppy, Ministry, KMFDM, D.O.A., GBH, The Offspring, Agent Orange, Nitzer Ebb, The Forgotten Rebels, The Pogues, The Ramones, The Clash, Sex Pistols, Front 242, Bigod 20, Front Line Assembly, Nine Inch Nails, White Zombie, Powerman 5000, The Sisters of Mercy, Sum 41, Billy Talent, Rise Against, Dropkick Murphys, A.F.I., Blink 182, Good Charlotte, Goldfinger, Linkin Park, The Misfits, and Treble Charger.

Thank you for hours of joy and hours more to come.

AUTHOR'S NOTE

SPECIAL THANKS to The Offspring, Alan Cross, and the Ongoing History of New Music. When I lived in Toronto, I loved listening to Alan Cross on CFNY 102.1, and his Ongoing History of New Music made for fascinating listening. Well over ten years ago (and possibly as many as twenty), I heard an anecdote about The Offspring's Dexter Holland and his education. The fact that he paused in his PhD program to focus on music was utterly fascinating. In September of 2016, I was driving along, listening to an Offspring song, and I started wondering if he ever went back to finish off his degree. And then the brain skipped, as it is wont to do, to a fully fledged idea, loosely inspired by that one question—did he go back to school? (I know the date, because I later jotted the idea down in my ever-increasing "ideas" folder.) I should probably emphasize… the idea and the story are not in any way supposed to represent The Offspring or any of the band members. They merely provided inspiration. Anyway, I pitched the idea to Dreamspinner in March 2017, and on June 2, 2017, as I was finishing up the manuscript, I decided to look it up. Imagine my surprise to find he'd been awarded his PhD on May 12, 2017. Go serendipity!

Chapter One

"Wake up, Devlin. It's getting late."

His mother's sharp tones rocketed him out of sleep, but he wasn't in his old bed, twenty-five years ago and late for school. Neither was he in his enormous bed in the main house. He was on his mother's couch, which wasn't nearly wide enough to keep him from rolling to the floor in a startled, confused tumble.

"Honestly, kid." His mother's tone became softer. "You okay there?"

Hardly a kid, but he didn't expect he'd break her of the habit at this late date.

Devlin flipped a tangle of sandy brown hair out of his eyes and gazed up at his mom, perfectly dressed and coiffed and ready for some luncheon or fund-raiser or something. "Fine, Mom." Except for an extreme case of embarrassment. Over his forty-one years, his mother had witnessed much worse, but it was still somewhat pathetic to have fallen off the damn couch, especially when he didn't have inebriation or a hangover to blame.

"You realize you have a perfectly good bed at your own house, right?" Her upper lip twitched as she suppressed a laugh.

He nodded. Plenty of time to untangle his limbs and get sorted once his mom left. "I know." But everything he did in that drafty mausoleum of a house echoed, the reverberations of solitude almost painful.

"It's not even that far to walk. Even if you drank too much."

Over the past few years he'd gotten drunk more than he used to, even for a guy who'd spent more than twenty years fronting a band, but he didn't think he'd ever been so blind, stinking drunk that he couldn't find his way from his mom's place to his house. That was the whole point of having her live in the guesthouse.

"Didn't drink. Just… fell asleep watching *Galaxy Quest*."

A discreet sniff from his mother might have been annoying, but she was still his mom, and she'd never liked him lying. When her nose wrinkled anyway, his cheeks burned in further humiliation. How long had it been since he'd showered last? If he never went anywhere besides his mom's place and his house, showering seemed an unnecessary expenditure of effort.

His mother's temporary amusement faded into worry, and that jabbed him with guilt. "Sorry, I forgot to shower, but I'll get on that right away."

She sucked in a breath, like she was going to say something, but let it out slowly. She didn't really need to say it, because he knew damn well what she was going to say. And he knew she was right. He also hated to worry her.

"I'm going to start going through those boxes in the basement today."

The worried look fled. "Finally. I swear that stuff is attracting vermin."

Dev rolled his eyes. If nothing else, he paid a groundskeeper and housekeeper plenty to ensure there weren't any unsanctioned vermin in either of their houses, but she thought it would be "good for him" to sort through all his old stuff. Cathartic or some such shit. But if it would ease the pinched lines of concern around her lips, then it was the least he could do. He'd pretty much binged all the television shows he was interested in anyway and had started working his way through some pure dreck.

"I'm not sure when I'll be back. I've got a full day of committee planning meetings, and Gail mentioned she might like to go out for dinner after the meeting. Will you be able to manage?"

Two years ago he would have huffed in exasperation. He was a grown man, middle-aged even, and could look after himself. But over the past six months, he hadn't given anyone the impression that he could, in fact, look after himself. Not well, at any rate, so he could hardly blame his mother for the question.

"I'll be fine, Mom. Pizza delivery is the number-one app on my phone." At least she wasn't aware—yet—of his doctor telling him he needed to start eating better or he'd be facing cholesterol meds.

“Tomorrow I’ll cook. Something healthier than pizza.”

“Sure, Mom. Sounds good.” But his mom had a brand-new social life he’d never known about until they started living in close proximity to each other. More than likely she’d be canceling or rescheduling some dinner or other to baby her son. Her forty-one-year-old son. She deserved the opportunity to be happy. Dev just wished he knew how she’d moved on when he couldn’t bring himself to do the same.

“Be good. I’ll see you later, kid, although you might want to give your own bed a whirl tonight. Sleeping on the couch can’t be good for your back. And you need your sleep.” The expression on her face was nothing less than mischievous. “Tonight’s a school night, after all.”

In a swirl of Chanel, she was gone, leaving Dev as stunned as if she’d punched him in the face.

School night. Surely she couldn’t mean what he thought she meant.

Dev waited until he heard the garage door close—her little hybrid was too quiet for him to hear its engine—before he tried to get up.

“Oh fuck.” He ached, and it felt like he’d hyperextended his knee. It was either the couch or the fall. He stumbled into the kitchen, muscles tense all over.

After emptying the grounds from the coffee maker, left over from his mother’s morning brew, he prepared another pot for himself.

With some caffeine in his system, he sat at his mother’s kitchen table and grabbed her calendar. Some of her clients provided free calendars as a promotional service, and she’d been using them faithfully for as long as he could remember. Birthdays, anniversaries, appointments—more doctors now than the Little League games that had filled his youth—appeared in her strong hand. Sure enough, she’d clearly marked tomorrow as “School Starts” in exactly the same way she’d done every year from kindergarten to grade twelve.

How was it September already? He wasn’t drinking steadily and yet somehow managed to lose the past few months to… television and video games. He huffed out a bitter laugh. Income from the band

and his savings meant he wouldn't have to worry about money, but right at this moment? He was an unemployed middle-aged man who slept most nights on his mother's sofa.

But he was no longer Blade, the gritty singer and bassist for the punk-industrial-goth band Negative Impression. Negative Impression died six months ago with their guitarist Trent, more commonly known as Reaver. The part of Dev that made up Blade had died alongside him. Now he was just Devlin Waters, unemployed and about to go back to university.

These days he had enough money to blow it off and not worry about the loss, but he'd disappointed his dad those many years ago when he'd dropped out after only a year. Not that his dad hadn't ultimately been proud of what Dev made of himself, but his father passing a few years ago made him want to erase that disappointment. Hitting his forties had been the impetus to reapply to finish his degree, although he'd intended to attend part-time while he continued recording and touring with the band.

When Trent died and Dev realized there was no way he could face music without his best friend, he'd changed his application to full-time, paid the required additional tuition, and then zoned the fuck out, more or less forgetting about the whole thing.

He was too old for this shit, but what else did he have to do with his life?

JACK JOHNSON strode into the lecture hall at a brisk clip. He was a few minutes late, and he didn't want the wretched frosh in their first year at university to buy into the fifteen-minute myth/urban legend and take off before he had a chance to hand out the syllabi for the year. Then again, it wasn't like attendance was mandatory at any class, so if the whole class decided to fuck off, it just meant Jack had more time, and the students were more likely to fail.

Sanji, one of the teaching assistants for this course, gave him a hard look from his place in the front row. He rolled his eyes.

"Good morning. This is Intro to Archaeology. I'm Dr. Jack Johnson. Normally this class is taught by Professor Nadine Redmond, but as she is on parental leave for the next several weeks, I'll be teaching you lot of miscreants."

His grouchy words got a few titters from the students, but he hadn't been trying for humor. He was happy for Nadine, he really was, but he was annoyed that he'd been assigned to cover the class, in addition to his normal workload. Intro to Archaeology sucked donkey eggs, and he didn't have Nadine's love of "nurturing the next crop of budding archaeologists, getting them excited about prehistory." Absolute garbage. If they managed to make it to university and not realize archaeology was one of the most interesting academic disciplines, then it wasn't up to him to correct that oversight. There were already too many students in this class, and this might be the worst year possible for him to have an overloaded schedule.

"Sanji, here, will be handing out the syllabus for this year." Jack handed Sanji the stack of papers—and the reason he was late. Sanji waved at the students as he stood. "Sanji is one of your teaching assistants, as is Meredith." She also stood and waved before Jack continued.

"In case you weren't paying attention when you registered, classes will be here, Monday and Wednesday at 9:00 a.m. sharp, unless there are holidays or other breaks, according to the official university schedule. Each of you should also have signed up for one hour of practical lab work each week, which may be guided by either myself, Meredith, or Sanji. There are several sessions—"

He broke off as the door opened, and in strode a man who was clearly not a brand-new first-year university student.

"Sorry I'm late." The man gave him a rueful grin but didn't sound terribly apologetic.

"Do try to be on time in the future." Jack's scolding didn't faze the man a bit. He merely wiggled fingers in Jack's direction as he slid into an open seat in the second row. Meredith leaped up and hand-delivered a syllabus. Undeserved attention for a student who was late.

With a barely smothered grimace, Jack turned his attention back to his notes. He did not like being interrupted.

"Where was I? Oh yes. Lab sessions will take place on Thursday or Friday starting next week."

God willing, he'd only be doing the labs for a couple of weeks.

"How many of you have seen the Indiana Jones movies?" Pretty much the whole class put their hands up. Hell, he hadn't even been alive when the first one came out. The students seemed to get younger every year, but that didn't diminish the almost timeless appeal of those movies. Or the timeless appeal of their star. Jack suspected his preference for older men might have germinated in his youthful crush on the ruggedly handsome Harrison Ford.

"How many of you think Indiana Jones is an accurate portrayal of an archaeologist… the most recent movie aside." Because there was an official term for an archaeologist who went around unearthing alien artifacts, and that name was "crackpot." Or perhaps "whackadoo" in more casual circles.

Far too many hands remained in the air, and he scowled at them. Honestly. Critical thinking was a lost fucking art.

"Well, I've got some bad news for you. There may have been a time when people barely above grave robbers called themselves archaeologists. And they behaved alarmingly like our charming Dr. Jones. Archaeology uses science, gold and gems are as rare as getting struck by lightning, and treasure doesn't tell us nearly as much about prehistoric societies as do garbage dumps."

Which was precisely the reason this class filled up every goddamn year, and the attrition rate was so high. Halfway through the semester, they'd be lucky to have half this many students. It meant a shit-ton of work in those first few weeks and months, though, until the exacting nature and the lack of glamor bored the idiots who thought they'd be slapping on a pith helmet, rifling through a grave or twenty, dodging spear-wielding natives, and scoring a solid gold idol, all in the first week. Indiana Jones might have been hot, but he was a grave-robbing maverick, at best.

At least the labs were scheduled in pairs so that as soon as attendance dropped, any of Jack's labs could merge into Sanji's or Meredith's equivalent, freeing up a few hours of his time. Unfortunately, depending on how determined this lot of frosh were, he might well be teaching labs until Nadine returned. Couldn't she be more traditional and take the full year's mat leave? But *nooo*, she had to split the parental leave with her husband, and that meant he was temporarily covering, rather than shuffling the entire schedule or course offerings for a full year.

"Now that you know what not to expect… the required text is listed on your syllabus. I expect everyone to have a copy before your first lab session, although if you wait until next week, you will be hopelessly behind." Jack continued on with the first day's lecture. Not much of a lecture, merely going over expectations, required reading for the next class, and an incredibly abbreviated history of the discipline.

Most of the first lecture he could deliver in his sleep, and a good thing too. Several times over the rest of the hour, Jack found his eyes wandering to the latecomer in the second row. By rights, in a class this full, he should never have found a seat so close to the front, but the rest of the "fresh out of high school" crowd seemed to have an ingrained terror of sitting too close to the front, and the damn lecture hall filled from back to front.

Mature students weren't uncommon, but usually it meant a couple of people his father's age interspersed in the sea of kids in their late teens. It had been a gift, because as yet, he'd had not one man who attracted him show up in any of his classes. Not any of his undergraduates. Some of his graduate students had held some appeal, but it hadn't been hard to avoid any impropriety.

This man, though, was going to be a distraction of the first order. A few years older than him, maybe as many as ten, sandy blond hair, freckles, laugh lines at the corners of hazel-colored eyes. Lean, fit, wearing jeans that lovingly cupped an ass made for sin, and a package that could tempt a saint. Something about his jawline and the sharp line of his nose gave Jack a frisson of déjà vu, but that had to be his mind playing tricks on him. No way could he have met and forgotten a man like that.

Jack Johnson might be a nerd, but he was no goddamn saint, and the sheer temptation of this man—this student—was going to make this class a million times more hideous. Last thing he needed was to battle a fucking hard-on in front of four-hundred-plus students. Nadine and her adorable cherub of a baby owed him large, and as soon as she got back, he'd collect.

Forty-seven excruciating minutes later, Jack excused the class and dashed out before anyone could tuck notebooks and laptops into bags.

CHAPTER TWO

HOLY FUCKING shit. Dev flopped back onto his bed and stared up at the ceiling. He had some totally interesting classes—even drunk and depressed he'd managed to find an assortment of classes that would not only exercise his brain but hopefully help him decide on a second career that didn't involve marathon Netflix sessions.

But he was going to have to work, and he hadn't truly worked in a long fucking time. Music was hard, touring was exhausting, and social media was like death to his soul, but fronting a successful band hadn't been a job. It hadn't been work. It had lived up to the adage "if you do something you love, you'll never work a day in your life."

Without Trent, though, music lost all its color, and he needed to find another occupation to love if he wasn't going to fritter away the second half of his life like a socially awkward hermit.

Showing up late for his very first class had been a little frustrating. Until that prickly, starched hottie of a professor had scolded him. Fuck, his cock had plumped right up, even as he ignored the admonition.

He wasn't a sub, or into the whole BDSM thing, but the occasional role-play with a stern teacher figure? Especially one that looked like Dr. Jack? Yes fucking please.

For all that the man dressed like a weedy librarian, he had the exact look Dev had determinedly aped as the lead of a punk-industrial band. Dev had to constantly keep up with his roots to keep his hair the glossy raven black Dr. Jack sported naturally, and no matter how many brands he tried, Dev could never find contacts that gave him Dr. Jack's clear blue irises. His skin was clear and pale, and he probably got fucking carded most places, even though he wasn't that much younger than Dev. Hell, even his lashes were thick, dark, and gave the illusion of faint guyliner.

Dev practically lived in mascara, thick black liner, and makeup to hide the freckles and the golden tan that appeared the moment he went outdoors. Freckles and sandy blond hair didn't suit the band, not at all. If Dr. Jack shaved the sides of his head and styled the rest of his wavy hair into a stubby Mohawk, he'd probably get mistaken for Dev during Negative Impression days. With his natural hair color and no makeup, it was the exceptionally discerning fan who'd recognize Dev, which was a blessing he'd never quite appreciated until now.

If only the class weren't at nine in the morning. Dev had never been much of a morning person, and while the whole registration process was a bit fuzzy, he couldn't believe he'd managed to sign up for interesting classes but hadn't managed to cram them all into the afternoon or evening.

But if he had, he might have missed the enigma that was Dr. Jack Johnson, and that would have been a crime. Sure, the professor might have been annoyed with him, but there was a reason he'd been a good front man for the band. He had charm, and he was bullheaded. He could probably get Dr. Jack to like him. If he couldn't, well, tweaking his nose, figuratively, would be an amusement in itself.

There were things he'd rather tweak, though. He'd have to keep an eye out for indications Dr. Jack played for his team. A number of times, his gaze had roved over Dev, but his "sucking on limes" sour expression made it hard to tell if Dr. Jack was attracted or held a grudge due to Dev's tardy arrival.

The hotness of his professor didn't distract him quite enough, though. Intro to Archaeology had only been the beginning, and by the end of the day, he wasn't sure how he was going to survive four years. Everyone else was so damned young. If he'd had any youthful indiscretions with a woman, he could have fathered just about any of his classmates. He'd pretended the assessing looks he'd gotten had been simple admiration of his appearance, but a good number of them had probably been wondering about his "mature student" status.

It was also a stark reminder that friends were in short supply, and the odds of finding any in this sea of Axe body spray and Proactiv acne treatment were—like Dr. Jack had said—less likely than getting struck by lightning.

He had a ton of homework, which was also fucking surreal. He'd taken a few basic courses when he and Trent were trying to get the band together, keeping his father partially mollified, but none of them twigged his interest. He was hoping the wide array of choices this time around would give him some guidance.

Which he should get started on, but he was crazy tired after figuring out where everything was on campus and hitting all his Monday classes. Stupidly, he'd set it up so Monday was his busiest day, and he suspected Mondays would shortly be on his shit list, even with the prospect of the delicious Dr. Jack first thing.

His phone buzzed, and as he reached to grab it, his stomach growled like an angry dog. Maybe he'd order in some food before he worried about homework.

Come over for dinner. I want to hear about your first day at school.

Dev huffed out a laugh. His mom might be committed to a paper calendar, but she'd grasped the fundamentals of smartphones just fine.

Be there in ten.

He set up his books and notes on his desk. If it weren't for his staff, he'd have had to dust the top off. It had been months if not years since he'd last used the thing.

With a fingertip he stroked the archaeology text. If he thought he could rile up the sexy Dr. Jack by not doing his homework, he'd probably skip it, but he suspected he couldn't gain anything but a shitty grade. Even if Intro to Archaeology took place at a simply unholy hour, Dr. Jack and his lecture had intrigued him enough that he was going to give it a real shot.

DEV SLID into his customary place at the kitchen table while his mom puttered at the stove. A giant bowl of tossed salad already sat in the middle of the table. He really needed to get a handle on his self-absorption, since he should be taking care of his mom and not the other way around, but when he moved back to Oakville, it didn't seem as though she needed taking care of. And he had to admit, there was the definite appeal—at any age—of letting a mom do all the worrying. His mom had been super young when she'd married his dad, and Dev had been born five months after their wedding, so at least he didn't have the added guilt of her age on top of everything.

"How's the charity committee going?"

His mother turned to him and stuck out her tongue, making Dev laugh. "Hallie Marsden is going to drive me to violence one day, I swear. Nitpicking on every idea, when everything she comes up with will cause twice as much work and cost three times more."

"They do say committees are the work of the devil."

His mom slid two plates of macaroni and cheese from scratch on the table and sat down across from Dev. Although they were both aware of the empty space where his dad would have sat, it didn't cause the same searing pain it used to.

"They do, do they? Whoever 'they' are, they've got some brains."

Dev scooped a forkful of pasta into his mouth and hummed in pleasure. When he was a kid and his parents were both labored with the effort of continuing their education while parenting an excitable, energetic kid, a lot of their macaroni and cheese came out of a blue box. His mom had been so proud the day she'd had the time to make mac and cheese from scratch, and it had quickly become one of the family's comfort foods.

The first day at university for a forty-one-year-old shouldn't require comfort food, but somehow it was exactly perfect.

"How'd it go?" His mother carefully looked down at her plate, like she was afraid Dev was close to having a meltdown and she didn't want to trigger him by being too solicitous.

"*Mooommm*. The other kids don't like me, and I don't have any friends." He intentionally made his voice super high and extra whiny.

That brought her head up, and she glared at him, which only made him laugh. "You little punk."

Dev only laughed harder. Since he'd spent decades fronting an actual punk band, that particular epithet didn't really hold up, and she knew it.

"Seriously, though, it is weird. Those kids are… kids. There are other mature students around, but how much would I have in common with them?" His lifestyle had certainly been atypical since Negative Impression had started touring in earnest, and he sort of had the feeling most people his own age were… not stick-in-the-muds, precisely, but had more in common with his parents than him. Besides, the majority of the people in his age group at university were faculty, not students.

"Well, I bet those mature students are also developing a second career. You might find more in common than you think."

A second career. The words sent white-hot pain searing through him, leaving him breathless. His mother made it sound so prosaic, when it was merely a desperate attempt to figure out who he was without the band or Trent to keep him grounded.

His mother grabbed his hand and squeezed. "I'm serious, Devlin. Your outside interests or career paths might not be the same as most people, but some of those people might also be embarking on a second career because of something catastrophic. Like we both are."

Dev took a deep breath and pulled his hand away. His mother had been adamant that he see a grief counselor, and he didn't want to hear her reasons again.

"Fine. I'll try to talk to someone. Labs and such start next week. It should be easier to strike up conversations then." He wouldn't mind chatting up the sexy Dr. Jack, but that probably wasn't what his mother had in mind.

His mother let out an aggrieved sigh, but Dev had every intention of procrastinating. For at least a week.

"Are there groups you could join?"

Dev rolled his eyes. "Even if I were still a pimply-faced teen, can you honestly see me doing that?"

She shrugged. "People change, Dev. Don't discount it out of hand. I'd be willing to bet there are a lot more social awareness groups than the last time you attended university. There might be something that aligns with the charities you support. And I can tell you with some authority that having something to do is a big help."

"And you don't think studying is enough?"

"Dev, honey, I love you to pieces, but you need people in your life, and studying is not social enough. What about Luke and Mo? I'm sure they'd love to see you."

Panic closed his throat. He hadn't seen either of them since Trent's funeral. Instead, he'd dodged their calls and put off answering any emails that didn't pertain to business. Even business emails he forwarded to his manager. He was not ready to see them, to commiserate with them, or even share stories about Trent. Just, no. Luke Baldwin, their keyboardist, known as Dragon, was too emotional, and Mo Khan, aka Snake the drummer, always had eyes filled with pity.

In the silence of his own heart, he could admit he was still too fucking fragile to face the hole in his life, but he could also admit he was arrogant enough to want to avoid confirming that fact for anyone else.

"I'll think about it." But socializing with strangers who were young enough to be his kids would be infinitely easier than being forced to confront Mo and Luke.

Like they'd had his mother's kitchen bugged, a message from Mo lit up his phone.

You can't ignore us forever.

Dev cleared the message. He could try; he could be a stubborn asshole when he wanted to be.

"Who was that?" There wasn't any sharpness in his mother's tone; she must not have seen who the message was from.

"No one."

Another message came through seconds later, from Luke.

Please call us. Email. Something.

Variations of the same messages he'd been receiving for the past six months. He turned off his phone. Talking about this with his mother was painful enough. The paper bag holding his shit together was practically translucent, and the knives of grief were only temporarily at bay. If he so much as saw his bandmates, the knives would go to work, spewing his emotional trauma everywhere and destroying his precarious state of mind. Avoidance was the only solution, and he'd do so for as long as it took.

For the rest of the meal, his mother took pity on him and spoke only about the fund-raisers she was working on, letting him eat in peace. But he'd never been so happy to escape his mother's company to go home and study.

JACK MADE it to Intro to Archaeology before the teaching assistants, for which he gave himself a mental pat on the back. He was well aware that his dislike of having to teach the class would have him dragging his feet most days, so arriving on time was a bit of a success.

It had nothing to do with the fluttery feeling in his stomach whenever he brought to mind that one student. Smug asshole.

Jack scrubbed his face with his hands. The last thing he needed was to develop any sort of infatuation with a student, but the guy's insolent arrogance infuriated Jack as much as it appealed to him, in a very visceral manner.

The first few students filtered into the room, and Jack smoothed his hair down before pulling out his notes for the second class, spreading them across the lectern.

Best-case scenario—Jack's little speech to discourage wannabe grave robbers meant that the cocky shit had dropped out already. The niggle of disappointment would not be acknowledged. It wasn't as if Jack hadn't ever tangled with men like that. He'd slept with the most arrogant man he'd ever met, and it had been awful. Not the sex. The sex had been world-class. But everything else about that encounter made it one of his most disappointing memories.

Jack gritted his teeth. He did not need to be thinking about sex minutes before a lecture.

Sanji arrived with a wave and approached him. "Meredith and I have a bet. She says your lecture last week scared off 5 percent of the students, I said 10."

That surprised a laugh out of Jack. "That boring, was it?" Good. His intention was to flush out everyone who wasn't serious, although he hadn't expected the attrition to be quite that significant. It usually took the first few practical sessions to "encourage" dropouts.

"Like you didn't do that on purpose." This wasn't the first time he'd worked with Sanji, but he definitely had more patience for the intro courses than Jack did; no surprise Nadine snapped him up for this course.

Jack shrugged. "Some secrets aren't meant to be shared."

Sanji chuckled and sat in the front row; Meredith joined him a moment later and smiled at Jack.

It took all of another thirty seconds to decide showing up late made more sense. Watching the students file in made him jittery as he eagerly searched each face for that one man who'd pissed him off and intrigued him in equal measure.

Someone like that wouldn't have what it took to stick it out in Jack's class. Searching for him was futile and pathetic. Resolutely he stared down at his notes, although he didn't really need them. From the sounds of chatter, feet stomping, and the shuffling sounds of asses hitting chairs, he hadn't scared away nearly as many students as he'd hoped. Certainly not the 10 percent his TA was gambling on.

Today's stratigraphy lecture would go a long way to help. Absolutely necessary and duller than dirt without potsherds.

Glancing up, he waited another minute as the last stragglers made their way to seats. Running his gaze quickly over the audience, he confirmed his suspicions. That guy from Monday hadn't shown. And no one had to know about the disappointment he swiftly and ruthlessly smothered.

"Good morning. Please settle down. We're going to get started."

"Good morning." That guy… here he was again. Sauntering in like he owned the place, self-satisfied smirk on his face. Then he had the absolute gall to sit in the front row but remained near the door as though ready for a quick escape at the end of the hour—or sooner. Jack glared, hoping to convey his irritation with such a lackadaisical attitude.

Then the guy winked at Jack, and every thought in Jack's head fled like rabbits chased by wolves. He cleared his throat and shuffled his papers. Someone had clearly swapped his notes for ones written in ancient Sumerian. What the fuck was wrong with him?

He coughed, nerves making it hard to swallow. Jack might not be the most confident when it came to picking up men in bars, but he hadn't been nervous in front of a class of students since his first day as a teaching assistant, back during his own graduate studies. One man shouldn't have this sort of effect, no matter how irritating or attractive he might be.

"Right. Let's get started." He bit back a groan. He'd already said that. Staring hard at his notes, they finally resolved into English.

It took a couple of sentences while averting his eyes from the left side of the lecture hall to get back on track. Stratigraphy was a vital premise for archaeologists, as it provided provenance for any items they found, but as lecture topics went, it was a far cry from golden statues and cursed amulets that everyone seemed to expect from archaeology. In other words, yet another tool in the arsenal for thinning the herd.

Jack allowed himself to think he was in control again. Then he made the mistake of glancing to the left. His nemesis slouched in his chair, legs spread, package encased in skintight denim. Blood roared into Jack's ears so fast he half expected them to ignite.

He wrenched his gaze out of his student's groin, only to find those intent hazel eyes staring at him, while he tapped a pen against sharply defined rosy lips. Those lips pursed, ever so slightly, but the tiny muscle shift was enough to suggest a million filthy and beautiful images.

Fuck, fuck, fuck.

Jack dropped his gaze to his notes so fast a streak of pain sliced through his temples, and the lecture stuttered to a stop as he tried desperately to remember what he'd been saying.

This had never happened to him before. No, not entirely true. He'd been captivated like this before—once. But not with a student.

A couple of deep breaths calmed him. He'd been lecturing a long time, and he was far too professional to let one ordinary, beautiful, irritating, sexy, damned *student* disturb his calm.

"As I was saying," Jack picked up again.

He managed to get through about ten minutes of the planned lecture by simply pretending the left edge of the room didn't exist, but the arm waving in his peripheral vision was a sign from above that his brittle peace wasn't going to last.

Reluctantly he turned his attention to his left. As he suspected, his nemesis was the one trying to get his attention. "Question?"

"Yes. Dr. Jack?"

Jack gritted his teeth. Not even for the pleasure of that smoky voice would Jack excuse such a transgression. "It's Dr. Johnson, Professor Johnson, or simply Professor. Not Dr. Jack."

Dr. Jack. For fuck's sake, made him sound like he was hawking penis-enlargement pills on a talk show.

"What about 'sir'?"

The word sent heat coursing through Jack's entire body, and he gripped the lectern in an effort to disguise his reaction in front of hundreds of witnesses. He couldn't even be certain his nemesis realized how intensely Jack was affected; for all Jack knew, this man was casually flirtatious in every situation. Certainly his proficiency spoke of a lot of practice.

Jack dragged in a breath, hoping he merely looked irate as he ignored the provocation. "What was the question?" And it better not be about calling him "sir."

"What's your field of study?"

Despite his goal of weeding out the nonserious students, he didn't want to discourage true interest. He hadn't completely lost sight of the reason he took on this career. He just wished he could tell if this question was sincere.

"My field of study is the emergence of complex societies in Mesoamerica."

Sandy eyebrows rose, and he chuckled, deepening laugh lines around those tempting lips. "And what's that when it's at home?"

Chastened, Jack dialed back his own arrogance and answered the question honestly, making an effort to describe what sort of things interested him about his own studies.

"You've all heard of Mayans and Incas, right? They had complex societies, and I study the factors that lead to the development of those types of societies."

Questions followed, fast and furious and not entirely from his nemesis. Before he knew it, he'd spent the rest of the hour talking about his own work and somehow not managing to mention stratigraphy once. He'd just have to make sure he kept on track next week when he dragged out the stratigraphy lecture again.

"Remember, class, lab sessions don't begin until next week, but please make sure you've read chapter ten."

Everyone filed out, including Sanji and Meredith, both of whom had given him quizzical looks for the entire length of his deviated lesson. Jack slapped his briefcase on the desk beside the lectern, the sound echoing through the empty lecture hall, and his shoulders relaxed. Talking about his field of study usually wasn't entertaining for anyone not in the same discipline, but Jack wouldn't have spent so much time and money on his degrees if he didn't find it all fascinating. He enjoyed talking about his work and teaching related courses to more experienced students, but the tension his nemesis caused never went away. Jack was far too aware of the man and his reactions to all of Jack's words.

Dr. Jack indeed. Hopefully he nipped that nonsense in the bud. Unfortunately, he feared he'd done nothing to lessen the class load—next week's lab sessions were going to be a giant pain in the ass.

CHAPTER THREE

JACK PICKED at the label on his beer bottle, letting his friends' banter wash over him without really listening.

His best friend, Stephanie, nudged him. "You doing okay?"

He shrugged. "Yes. Maybe. I'm restless today." Normally practice days were a great outlet for stress, but even after two hours, preparing for a Saturday-night gig hadn't settled him.

"You really nailed 'Crimson in the Vein' today," Stephanie observed.

Jack snorted and rolled his eyes. He loved being in the band, but he certainly wasn't a required component. Between the two of them, Stephanie was the real musician. They'd met during orientation at the University of Toronto and bonded over their love of a somewhat obscure band, Negative Impression. Twenty years ago, Jack had been an angry, lonely teenager, drawn to dark sounds and angry music. Back then, Jack had always worn black, wore thick eyeliner, and had a perma-scowl. He listened exclusively to punk, goth, and industrial music, and Negative Impression managed to blend all three, in addition to being local. By the time Jack was old enough to attend concerts at bar venues, Negative Impression had moved on to touring almost exclusively in Europe and the US. The few times they played in Toronto, Jack tried to make it to all of their shows.

Nevertheless, he'd met a kindred spirit in Stephanie. They'd grown close, and even though his father had hated the "theatricality" of it all, he'd held out hope that Stephanie would "cure" Jack of his gayness.

About seven years ago, when Stephanie joined a cover band called Crimson Corrosion that played primarily Negative Impression songs, Jack had been thrilled and made a point of attending all their gigs. None of the band members had expected to make a living at it; it was merely a way to celebrate a band and style of music they loved. About a year after Stephanie joined, Jack joined as the vocalist. Barry wanted to focus on just the guitar parts and gratefully gave up the singing part to Jack. Just as well. Jack dabbled on the guitar, but he didn't have the skill to play full sets or mimic the music of Reaver, Negative Impression's late guitarist. Singing he could do, and until recently, he'd been in absolute awe of Blade, the band's vocalist and bassist.

Maybe it didn't matter. They were all friends and had fun.

"First week of school always sucks, doesn't it?" Stephanie shook her head. "You need to take a sabbatical or something. Get down into the Yucatan and do another dig. After you've spent six months grubbing about in the dirt, you'll be a lot less grumpy."

Jack nodded. "Perhaps." He did miss fieldwork, but he'd also enjoyed lecturing. Most times. With his dad in assisted living, waiting for a spot in a long-term care facility that could cope with the aggression exacerbated by the Alzheimer's eating away at his brain, Jack certainly couldn't make plans like that. "Maybe I just need to get laid."

Barry leaned in and leered. "Yeah, you do." Trust Barry to hear the part of the conversation about sex. "Honestly, I don't know how you're not getting laid daily. You have honest-to-God groupies at our gigs, and you're surrounded daily by hot, young university students. Don't you just have to snap your fingers to get some tail?"

Ann, their bassist, smacked Barry's arm, making him howl with indignation. "God, you're a pig."

"I'm not supposed to view my students as a sexual smorgasbord. They frown on that, you know." Most times, he didn't even find his students attractive. But then, most of his students were younger than he liked. One of the exceptions, though…. Jack wouldn't mind feasting on him.

He gulped at his beer to try and cool the sudden flames in his cheeks.

Stephanie's eyes narrowed. "You've got someone in mind, don't you?"

"No. Of course not. My love life is drier than the Sahara."

"It *is* the beginning of the year. No new student or teaching assistant caught your eye?"

Jack squirmed under her regard. “There’s no one.” That arrogant asshole might be pretty to look at, and had maybe fueled a couple of fantasies already, but that’s as far as Jack was willing to go, even if the guy was gay and had been seriously flirting with Jack. Which he doubted. Men like that just enjoyed the conquest; they used people, uncaring of anyone’s feelings. Jack had learned his lesson already.

Kirk, the band’s drummer, spoke up. “You sure? You could invite them to the show next week.”

“No, I don’t think so.”

Most of Jack’s students would probably be amazed if they knew the type of music he preferred, and sure as shit his nemesis wouldn’t be interested. His nemesis, if he were interested in dating, looked like a jock, who probably listened to classic rock or something. Maybe even grunge—he was the right age. But he doubted he’d be interested in a Negative Impression cover band.

Jack pressed his lips together. Even considering the possibility of dating that man was setting himself up for disappointment and misery. How could it not? A man like that would only be interested in one night. Jack had already done that and wasn’t interested in repeating it. He could get used to celibacy. Not like he hadn’t been practicing like he was planning to enter the priesthood.

“Surely there are more interesting things to talk about than the possibility of dating my students.”

Barry snorted. “If you don’t want to, I will.” Ann rolled her eyes. For all of Barry’s coarseness, though, he was nothing more than a softhearted bear. If he was gay, Jack would have asked him out. Alas, life was never that simple.

Maybe it was time to dust off a dating app or two. Problem was, he wanted to get to know someone intellectually before baring dicks, but that seemed to be a minority on the apps. Clubs that played music he didn’t hate often weren’t great for picking up other guys—he just wasn’t a Lady Gaga, Beyoncé, Taylor Swift gay guy.

God. He was one step from waving his fist around, yelling at the kids to get off his lawn. Old and curmudgeonly before his time.

He definitely needed to get laid.

JACK PRINTED out the attendance lists for his fourth and last lab session of the week for his Intro class. He'd been lucky. His nemesis hadn't been in any of the previous three labs, and he hoped his luck held for one more. Odds were good that he'd ended up in one of Sanji's or Meredith's labs, and he shouldn't worry, but fuck. That guy had made it his life's work to mess with Jack's head.

Each class had been a torment. That guy sat in the front row and continued to ask questions. Jack had managed to keep his answers concise, but he was losing patience. The questions sprang from a true interest from someone who had absolutely no relevant knowledge, or they were designed to throw him off-balance. Jack leaned toward the latter, especially since he couldn't keep the guy from calling him Dr. Jack. Bastard. Jack had desperately wanted to ask his name so he could ensure he ended up in one of his TAs' labs, but he was afraid he couldn't ask without giving something away. Bad enough he'd… dammit. He wasn't going to think about how he'd drunk a couple glasses of wine at his condo, then jacked off thinking about the man.

This was getting ridiculous. It was Friday. As soon as he taught this lab, he was done for the day, done for the week. He messaged one of the more promising men he'd been chatting with this past week. He needed a date. Something to get his mind off his student.

A gratifyingly short time later, Matt aka hotbod35 agreed to meet for drinks. Immediately on the heels of that was a text from Stephanie.

Brunch with me and Ian on Sunday?

Jack laughed ruefully. His social life was looking up.

Sure. Let me know when and where.

He'd probably be slogging out to Oakville. Stephanie might still look every bit a goth princess, but she'd gotten married and moved out to the burbs with her hubby. No one would ever think it just to look at her, but she loved gardening, and finding a place in downtown Toronto with a decent patch of green in which to garden was next to impossible.

Eh. Oakville had its charms, not the least of which was Stephanie herself. Jack lived in fear of a pregnancy announcement. He wasn't ready for that much of a disturbance in the Force, but he suspected Stephanie wanted kids. Her rebellious phase was long over. Hell, he'd long since given up on the shoddy, tiny apartments available in the downtown core, trading in a longer commute for a bigger space, decent parking, and better pest control near the end of the subway line. If he never saw another cockroach again, it would be too soon.

Sanji knocked on his open door, and Jack glanced up. "Ready?"

"As I'll ever be." Jack handed over Sanji's attendance list, gathered up his notes and his own attendance list, and followed Sanji to the elevator.

He quickly scanned the list of names, his gaze lingering on the last one. Devlin Waters.

Clammy sweat slicked his palms, and he swallowed heavily. "Huh. That's funny." In a "the universe is fucking with you" sort of way.

"What's funny?"

"One of my students for this session. His name is Devlin Waters."

Sanji looked at him blankly, but no surprise there.

"Ever hear of a band called Negative Impression?" Negative Impression had done well for themselves, although they never had the mainstream popularity that, say, Nine Inch Nails did, but Sanji surprised Jack.

"Yeah. Kinda hard-core local band, right? Did fairly well." He gave Jack a quizzical look. "I'm sort of astonished you know them."

Jack's cheeks flushed. He'd never needed to dye his hair or wear any makeup besides eyeliner to fit into the goth crowd, but he was well aware that most people thought he was nothing more than a boring, stodgy professor. As yet, Crimson Corrosion hadn't crossed paths with his colleagues or anyone from his classes, but if it ever did, he'd probably shock a lot of people.

"Can't judge a book by its cover, you know." Jack tugged at the collar of his pale blue button-down. The preppy wardrobe put him in the right frame of mind, and honestly, he didn't care to lay too much personal stuff out there for his students.

"Fair enough. But why bring them up?"

He and Sanji got in the elevator and headed for the ground floor. Jack pointed to Devlin Waters on his list. "That's the name of the band's lead singer and bassist." Jack tried not to cringe.

"Really? I thought they all had pseudonyms, like… Blade, wasn't it?"

"Sure, but you don't think his parents actually named him Blade, do you?"

Sanji laughed. "Of course not. I guess you must be a real fan, though, if you know the guy's name."

Jack would bet his next month's pay that 90 percent of their fans didn't know the members' real names. They had embraced the pseudonyms wholeheartedly: Blade, Reaver, Dragon, and Snake. But Jack had been a super fan, hence the cover band. He'd dug deeper, and he knew all their real names. Not like they were truly hidden, but neither were they publicized.

An oily sensation of regret and shame made him queasy. This Devlin Waters couldn't be Blade. Jack would have noticed him.

"Do you think it's him?"

Jack scoffed. "What would the lead singer of Negative Impression be doing in Intro to Archaeology?"

Weird coincidence, but it had to be nothing more than that. If nothing else, at least he'd put his nemesis out of his mind for a few minutes.

He and Sanji parted ways halfway down the hall to go to their respective classrooms. Jack strode to the front of the much smaller lab room and faced a group of about twenty-five students. He swept his gaze over the lot of them, and not only was his nemesis not present, but neither was there a rock star who had at one point weakened Jack's knees and set his belly fluttering. Blade's coloring was similar to Jack's own, and while there were a number of black-haired students in the class, none of them had pale skin and hazel eyes.

Relief drained the tension out of his shoulders; he hadn't realized just how wired he'd gotten from reading that one name.

"Class, today we're going to look at soil types." Another boring yet necessary lesson. Honestly, the students didn't get to the good stuff in the first-year course at all, in Jack's opinion. Took a determined person to slog it out, and he suspected he'd be seeing a significant drop in registered students by Monday morning's class.

"First of all, unlike the lectures, attendance at the labs is part of your grade." Jack called out names in alphabetical order, until he finally came to the last name, but he didn't think there were any students unaccounted for.

"Afternoon, Dr. Jack." Jack gritted his teeth as his nemesis sailed into the room, like he wasn't late at all, and grabbed an empty seat next to a studious-looking blonde girl—Debbie Hoffman, if he recalled.

"Devlin Waters, I presume?"

"That's me."

Of course it fucking was. The universe was laughing at him. The coincidence was too fucking ridiculous. He'd have to tell Stephanie over brunch, although she didn't know the whole story. The one and only time he'd met his idol, Devlin Waters, aka Blade from Negative Impression, had been too humiliating to share with anyone.

Debbie Hoffman was going to end up doing all the work for Devlin, Jack was sure of it.

"Do try to be on time, Devlin. I won't be holding up the class for you."

Devlin merely smirked and waved a hand as though giving Jack permission to continue. What a dick. It wasn't fair that he was also so hot. At least now he had a name for the arrogant asshole, and he should have guessed that this was going to be Devlin Waters.

Before long, Jack shook off his disquiet and got the class working on their practical assignment. He wandered among the desks answering questions, observing, and prompting when necessary. He'd only been past Devlin's desk once and really ought to make another pass; he didn't want his avoidance to be obvious.

He rounded the desks at the left of the room, walked along the front, and approached Devlin's desk. Devlin casually rucked up his T-shirt and scratched at the bare skin of his belly.

Jack sensed Devlin smirking, but he couldn't tear his gaze away from the tattoo Devlin had exposed. It was an abstract symbol that Negative Impression had chosen as their logo, and the last time Jack had seen it, he'd traced it with his tongue before he'd gone on to swallow a hard, dripping cock.

His heart rate soared, and a clammy sweat broke out on the base of his spine. He dragged his gaze upward and stared at Devlin's face. A gray haze filmed over his vision as his lungs constricted.

Fuck. Fuckity fuck fuck. The coloring was all wrong, which had fooled Jack, but the features were the same. His fluid grace of movement was the same. The arrogance and insouciance he should have recognized immediately. There was no coincidence of two men with the same name causing havoc in Jack's life. There was only one. This one.

But there wasn't a shred of recognition in Devlin's eyes.

Light-headed, blood pounding in his ears, Jack tried to breathe. Was this a stroke? A panic attack?

"I'll be back in a moment." His voice didn't crack or wobble, for which he thanked all the deities that man had ever worshipped, and he fled the room as fast as he could without actually running. Out in the hall, he considered just dropping to the floor, but the restroom wasn't far, and he made a beeline for it.

Gulping in air, he leaned over the sink. This couldn't be happening. He'd never expected to see Devlin again. Never wanted to. Lusting over him as a student was too fucking surreal, and if he didn't know better, he'd think he was hallucinating. He gripped the porcelain, as ice-cold as his hands, and focused on breathing.

DEVLIN SAT there stunned. He'd been enjoying riling up the poised and perfect Dr. Jack just as much as he'd enjoyed the classwork. He had a number of anthropology courses, which were also extremely interesting, but Dr. Jack made archaeology an enigma. He'd gone out of his way to make the topic seem boring as shit, even though it was what he'd chosen to do with his life. Devlin could see the glaze of boredom on the faces of his fellow students, but Devlin didn't find it boring at all. It was like the glamorous idea people had of archaeologists: the fictional like Indiana Jones and Allan Quatermain, and even the real-life ones like Howard Carter were the finished item. The show. What Dr. Jack taught in his lessons was like building the backstage, setting up the audiovisual equipment and microphones. The endless rehearsals so the band could transition from one song to another without any hitches. The building blocks of creating a memorable concert. He wasn't an idiot—of course the Hollywood version had little resemblance to the real thing. That didn't mean the real things weren't fascinating on their own.

Boring to some, but Devlin had always enjoyed the details that went into the final product, possibly to the irritation of some of their roadies.

He'd also enjoyed the flared nostrils and dilated pupils Dr. Jack exhibited whenever he glanced Devlin's way. If he hadn't been sitting in the front row, he'd never have noticed. Whether he'd try and take it any further than a little classroom flirtation, that remained to be seen. Asking someone out at this point in his life might not be fair to either of them, and he wasn't entirely sure if half of his attraction was the chance to ruffle the feathers of the unflappable Dr. Jack. Poking authority in the eye made up the underpinnings of many of Negative Impression's songs. They weren't a popular underground group for nothing.

But he'd never wished anything bad to happen to Dr. Jack. Judging from his sudden pallor, Dr. Jack was not well. He had more than enough self-confidence to know the sight of his still-flat belly hadn't made Dr. Jack sick. The professor may or may not be out, and may or may not be pleased by his attraction to Devlin, but Devlin knew he revved Dr. Jack's engine. This was something different. Concerning.

Devlin glanced around the room. No one else seemed worried.

"Be back in a flash, Debbie." She smiled sweetly at him and bent her head back to their shared task.

He sped out of the room in time to see the men's room door slowly swing shut. Exactly what he'd expected.

When he stuck his head in the door, he half expected to hear the sound of retching, but instead Dr. Jack swayed by the sink, looking more like he was going to pass out rather than puke.

"Shit," he muttered. At least these bathrooms weren't festering sewers like some of the hole-in-the-wall clubs he'd played at back when Negative Impression was just starting out.

He slid in beside Dr. Jack, who smelled pretty fucking good, once he filtered out the acrid scent of commercial bathroom deodorizers.

Jack flinched, as though he'd just realized Devlin was there. Maybe he hadn't noticed until this second.

"C'mon, man. Let me help you sit down before you fall down."

"What?" Jack stared at him like he'd been speaking in tongues.

"You look like you're about to pass out. You need to sit down, maybe get your head between your knees."

"I'm fine." Jack blinked at him. "Shouldn't you be in class?"

Devlin rolled his eyes. "Dr. Jack…." The name put a couple of dots of color back in the man's cheeks. Good. "You looked rough for a moment." He grabbed Jack's hands and rubbed some warmth back into the strong, blunt fingers.

"What are you doing?"

"Feeling better? I wanted to make sure you were okay." The ghostly cast to his face slowly receded, but Jack wasn't exactly pleased. He looked conflicted, like he'd been offered a gift but wasn't sure it was meant for him. He tugged his fingers out of Devlin's grip and crossed his arms, still-chilly fingers pressed tightly to his sides.

Prickly. And something about that made Devlin want to disturb his quills all the time. Well, all the time except when Jack clearly wasn't well.

"I'm fine." Jack grimaced. "Thank you."

Inwardly, Devlin smirked. That tiny bit of gratitude sounded painful.

"You're welcome. Did you want me to walk you back to class?"

"That won't be necessary. I'll be along in a minute." Ouch. The prim and proper professor had returned. Sexy as hell, and Devlin had had enough sexual encounters in public bathroom stalls that if it weren't for Jack's lingering pallor, their proximity was almost foreplay.

Devlin was leaning more and more toward asking the man out. Although he'd been called the name more than once, he didn't really go out of his way to be an asshole. When Jack had recuperated, and once Devlin had a grip on his own motivations and limitations, he'd have a better idea if he wanted to date Jack or just engage in light, meaningless flirtation as student and professor. He wasn't gonna lie—the thought of that sort of role-play in the bedroom was fucking hot. Dr. Jack didn't strike him as a one-night stand or bathroom-blowjob sort of guy. Devlin didn't think he was either, but he didn't know for sure. No one had ever stuck around before, and he didn't know how to keep someone around. He certainly hadn't had a boyfriend long enough to role-play with them before.

For now, though, retreat was clearly the best option.

"Sure thing, Dr. Jack. But if you're not back in five minutes, I'm coming to look for you."

Jack sputtered, and Devlin sauntered out of the bathroom. He wasn't fucking kidding, though. If Jack truly were ill, he wasn't about to let the man collapse. This class was late enough on a Friday it was starting to feel like a ghost town. Devlin couldn't leave the man in a building that might not see another soul until Monday.

A few minutes later, Devlin helped Debbie finish up their practical exercise. He resolutely did not look up when he heard the measured steps of Jack returning. He'd be good, let Jack get his equilibrium back. Monday was soon enough for a little more flirtation.

Jack laughed nervously at Matt's terrible joke, garnering him a benevolent, pleased look. At least one of them thought this date was going well. Small talk wasn't a particular skill of his, and it had only been a few hours ago that he'd thought he was going to faint in the men's room in the Sanderson research wing. Devlin Waters, aka Blade, had even followed him, worried about him.

Another borderline-hysterical laugh bubbled up in his throat, but he held it in, waiting for the next appropriate anecdote to unleash it on. He didn't think he'd ever been so conflicted in his life, not even back when his father insisted he needed to do manly, sports-type things in order to… fuel his father's testosterone or something.

Devlin Waters. In all his guises, Jack was attracted, even as he hated him. Devlin showed today he wasn't an asshole of astronomical proportions, and yet Jack saw no glimmer of recognition, no understanding of exactly why Jack had freaked out. Bad enough that Devlin was single-handedly responsible for the most humiliating memory in Jack's arsenal, but Jack had managed to look like a complete idiot in front of him. Again. Deep in his psyche lurked some substantial masochistic tendencies, and not the sexy ones.

"Don't you think?" Matt stared at him expectantly, and Jack blinked at him, vaguely annoyed at the interruption to his internal musings. He was even more annoyed that Devlin was taking up so much of his brain time.

Unfortunately Jack had absolutely no idea what Matt had been talking about and did not have the verbal dexterity to get himself out of this hole. He stared back at Matt for one interminable moment, lips parted, brain devoid of a logical response. He could go with yes or no, but depending on what Matt had said, he could be getting himself in trouble.

The server sidled up to their table. "Can I get you another round of drinks?"

Jack had never been so happy to see someone in his life. "Yes, please. Can I try one of the merlots this time?" He didn't mind wine, but he obviously didn't care about it the same way Matt did, given his suggestion they meet at a wine bar and his intense perusal of the options. Fortunately their server figured out from their first round all the wine-speak was lost on Jack.

Once Matt had spent a few minutes talking—years, bouquets, and whatnot—the server left.

"Uh, so what was it you were saying again?" Now at least he had a good reason for his lapse.

Matt pursed his lips, and Jack frowned. Was he doing that on purpose to draw attention to his mouth? The gesture seemed a little exaggerated.

"I don't recall. I wish you'd let me choose a wine for you."

Jack raised an eyebrow. "Why? How would you even know what I'd like?"

There it was again. That faint sense of condescension.

"Maybe you wouldn't like it, but I could guide you to some fabulous choices. I've taken a number of courses, and I've been on wine-tasting trips to France and Italy. I'm sure we could find something you'd like."

Jack stretched his lips in an expression he hoped resembled a smile. If Jack cared enough about finding the bestest wines ever, he'd have taken courses too, but he didn't give a shit. Most wines tasted just fine to him, although he hated champagne and dessert wines. What else did he really need to know? He didn't even give a shit about matching red or white to beef or fish.

"Would you like to get dinner after this? I made dinner reservations at a restaurant down the street. The chef is supposed to be fantastic."

It took some effort to keep from rolling his eyes. Of course Matt would know things about the chefs at restaurants. Jack had grown up eating spaghetti, pizza, and takeout. Fine cuisine was tasty, but he often felt out of place in fancy restaurants. And since he'd spent the time between his fateful last class and this date hiding out in his office rather than going home and freshening up, he didn't feel like he was properly dressed.

"Sure, we could do that." If they did, Jack was going to find out what wine matched his entrée and he was going to order the exact opposite, just to see Matt's expression.

God. He really was becoming a curmudgeon. And he knew exactly what—or who—had put him in this unsettled, devilish mood.

For the first time, Matt appeared to hesitate. Jack mustn't have done a good enough job of hiding his disgruntlement. "Or we could grab something light from here and hit a club after?"

Matt wasn't perfect, but who was? Jack knew damned well he wasn't giving the man a fair chance, and Matt did seem invested in talking. Mostly about himself so far, but Jack had been too distracted to carry his share of the conversation.

Like he needed Devlin fucking his love life up more than he already had.

"How about we split the difference? Go to the place you made reservations—thank you for thinking ahead—and eat light there. Then we can go to the club."

He didn't expect he'd be a fan of the music, but maybe he could work off some of his agitation on the dance floor.

Matt smiled toothily at him. "Perfect. We've got plenty of time to finish our second glass of wine. Then we can walk to the restaurant."

This time Jack put some effort into telling Matt a little more about his career. He inspected Matt's features as they chatted. He was a few years older than Jack, and was pleasant to look at, but Jack couldn't help but wish he had the same opportunity to inspect Devlin's features.

He'd spent so many years mooning over pictures of, well, the entire band, but Blade was the one he had gravitated to most. He never once suspected there was a freckle-faced, towheaded boy-next-door under all the dyed black hair and makeup. It was possible that Devlin today was a result of artifice, but Jack suspected this was Devlin au naturel. Negative Impression did well for a Canadian band that never made mainstream music, and never really tried, although some of their songs broke into the charts. Regardless, their popularity was nothing that would require a full-on disguise just to go to university. Even at the pinnacle of their success, Devlin wasn't about to get mobbed by paparazzi—journalists and tabloids had bigger fish to fry than punk bands. And his natural coloring made extremely effective camouflage even with devoted fans. But Jack was missing out on the real Devlin. Although he shouldn't give a fuck. Not one single fuck, when there was a nice man in front of him, wanting to get to know him better.

Jack swallowed a sigh and jumped into the conversation. Jack was too old to be starstruck by an arrogant asshole. Even one he'd had a one-night stand with. Especially when Jack apparently hadn't been at all memorable.

By the time they were ready to settle up their bill at the restaurant, Jack felt a little better about the date. He probably should have just canceled, though, because he wasn't really in the mood. He also wasn't sure if Matt was the one for him. Obviously a few days of texting and one date wasn't enough to make that determination, but neither could he tell if Matt was just a nohoper. But since he'd already determined he wanted to get to know guys before jumping into bed with them and he'd finally made a concerted effort to use one of his dating apps, it only made sense to give it his best shot.

FUCKING HELL. Jack should have known, just by the overdressed patrons waiting in line, that this club wasn't going to be his scene. At all. Not only because he was still wearing work clothes and not club clothes. Nope. This was one of those übertrendy places that'd be nothing more than a memory in six months. A flash in the pan. Except Matt had also gotten them on the VIP list, and they bypassed the line. It had been a long time since someone had gone to any sort of effort to please Jack. He just wished the effort had gone to something that would *actually* be pleasing. Of course, that assumed Matt wasn't a pretentious prick who pulled these tricks on every first date to try and impress people.

Jack spent half his working life digging up artifacts in the jungle, covered in dirt and sweat and fecund plant material. He spent the rest of his career grumbling at lazy students. He was hardly the type that needed this sort of mating display.

Matt whisked him past the bouncer into the club. Blue lights strobed and streaked across the dance floor, providing a similar but softer effect than black lights. The club took full advantage, and neon straws, swizzle sticks, and umbrellas gleamed brightly, enticing everyone to indulge.

The music, though. Jack sighed and followed Matt to the bar. It was poppy and light. Cheery. Modern. And it utterly failed to sing to Jack's innermost heart. He hadn't entertained the possibility the club would play the darker music he preferred, but he'd hoped for at least some Erasure, or disco. Maybe some Donna Summer.

Not a chance. Jack sighed again as he waited for the bartender to head their way. He didn't need the man he ended up with to have the same musical tastes—although it would be nice—but if this was Matt's preferred jam, Jack foresaw a lot of separate socializing. Matt might go to a couple of Jack's gigs, but probably only in the beginning.

Not a deal breaker, but the cheery tunes sounded discordant to him. Negative Impression, and others with similar music, like KMFDM or Ministry… those were what got his hips moving. So many people didn't understand, but those were the bands that made him happy, that soothed him. They were his go-to.

But he'd try. He swore he'd try. And if this didn't work out, there were others hiding in his dating apps.

He'd been planning on just getting a bottle of water, but if he was going to stick it out for a reasonable amount of time, he'd need a little more than the wine that had been soaked up by dinner.

One vodka cranberry later, he and Matt edged closer to the dance floor. The song—which Jack and his satellite radio had only heard a couple of times—ended, and another one started. It involved a lot of squealing and hand waving and a throng of people mobbing the dance floor. Politely, though. Nary a slam dance to be seen.

Popular, clearly. Matt turned to him eagerly and tilted his head toward the dance floor.

"I'd like to finish my drink first."

"Are you okay if I go?"

"Of course." One of them might as well have a good time.

Matt thrust his drink at Jack. "Watch this for me, will you?"

Jack nodded, but the action surprised him. Roofies weren't reserved for girls, and Matt was putting a lot of trust in Jack, who was a virtual stranger. Lucky for Matt that Jack wasn't a giant douchebag.

He'd stick it out an hour, then claim a headache. With any luck Matt had taken him at face value and wasn't expecting Jack to put out. Because it wasn't happening, but Jack didn't want to deal with shooting down the suggestion.

Besides, Saturday was his day to visit his father, and doing it hungover didn't improve the experience any.

CHAPTER FOUR

JACK WAVED at Stephanie and wandered through the maze of tables at the chic Italian restaurant where they were having brunch.

"Ian not joining us?"

She rolled her eyes. "He had to run a few errands for his mom, but he should be here soon. We can be well into a couple of Bloody Marys before he shows up."

A girl after his own heart. Mimosas might be a typical brunch drink, but orange juice couldn't disguise the unpleasant tang of champagne.

"Oh good. I have to talk to you about something."

Stephanie eyed him speculatively while the server took their order. The moment the skinny, black-clad man departed, she leaned across the table.

"You're going to let me set you up."

"What? No. I mean… maybe?"

She wiggled in her seat. "Awesome."

Jack shuddered. He'd—apparently—been laboring under the misapprehension that he was able to find his own dates. Stephanie had been wanting to set him up for ages, and since he'd decided to launch himself out there, maybe it wouldn't hurt.

"But that's not what I meant."

"Wait… you were on a date Friday night. It went badly, then? Spill!"

He was going to have to duct-tape her mouth shut. "Steph, shut up a minute. I have to talk about this, but I can't tell you in front of Ian."

"You… is this a secret?"

Jack waved a hand. "Oh, you can tell him. I know you will anyway. It's just too embarrassing. Can you let me talk now?"

Stephanie mimed locking her lips and throwing away the key.

Now that he had her undivided attention, he wasn't sure where to start. He sucked in a deep breath. He had to start somewhere and soon, because he hadn't been kidding about not talking about this in front of her husband. Ian was one of those stoic, salt-of-the-earth types who've never made an ass out of themselves because they have no impulsive tendencies whatsoever.

"Remember for my thirtieth birthday you got me tickets for Negative Impression?" During university, they'd gone to see every show, but by the time Jack was thirty, it had been a while since he'd seen them.

She pouted theatrically. "Yes. Then I ended up getting pneumonia of all things and couldn't go with you."

Jack glared, but mildly. Stephanie wasn't one for staying quiet for any reason.

"Well, I didn't tell you everything that happened."

JACK BREATHED heavily. Sweat slicked his body. Negative Impression didn't play locally nearly often enough, considering they were a Toronto-based band. The concert had been fucking fantastic, though, and Jack had danced with the throng by the stage almost the entire set.

His belly might be a little soft—he was a fucking professor—but he kept himself in fairly good shape, and the night had been like a solid, endorphin-rich workout. He'd have preferred it if Stephanie had been well enough to come with him, but he'd done okay on his own. The bartender had flirted with him, and gave him heavy-handed pours.

It wasn't last call yet, and the music had switched over to a DJ. Perhaps a bit of a letdown after the electric energy of a live performance, but the music was good, Jack was still buzzed, and he was horny as hell. If he couldn't find someone who suited him better, he'd do his best to go home with the bartender.

He winked at the bartender, gulped down the last of his vodka and cranberry, then pushed his way back into the middle of the dance floor.

Several songs later the vibe on the dance floor changed, and Jack pulled himself out of his head to pay attention to his surroundings, only to see a familiar black Mohawk right in front of him.

His stomach clenched in dizzy anticipation. Blade was on the dance floor. Dancing. Right in front of him. Goose bumps sprang up along his nape, and he barely kept himself moving as Blade's sinuous hip movements ensorcelled him.

A quick glance around the room showed the rest of the band—Reaver, Dragon, and Snake—were all on the dance floor, each with a coterie of admirers knotted around them.

Jack returned his attention to Blade, because it was only a matter of time before Blade moved on. Then Blade looked him right in the face and licked crimson-painted lips.

Suddenly, Jack was no longer a thirty-year-old professor of archaeology. In the time it took him to suck in a shocked breath, he'd become a teenager with a crush. A serious crush that he'd never really lost.

Thick black eyeliner ringed hazel eyes, and Jack thought he just might drown in them. Blade danced closer, a tiny grin curling the corners of his mouth, hips moving hypnotically, like a cobra luring in its prey.

And Jack was willing prey.

His breath came short, and he couldn't stop staring. Blade pressed their bodies together and nosed under the untidy flop of Jack's black mane to get to his ear. "I noticed you in the audience. What's your name?"

Jack froze for a second. "Jack," he gasped out.

Then Blade licked his ear.

Oh fuck. Electricity streaked from his earlobe directly to his dick. He was hard, aching, and light-headed. Asking how or why might pop the bubble of this particular mirage, and Jack wasn't stupid enough to do that.

A strangled moan escaped his lips; he had no ability to form actual words.

"Want to spend the night with me?" Blade issued the invitation against his ear, lips tickling his skin, before biting his neck, and Jack nearly creamed himself right there on the dance floor.

"Oh God, yes."

WITHIN MINUTES a limo whisked them, the rest of the band, and their chosen companions away to a nearby hotel.

Jack spent a solid thirty seconds wondering why none of the band members had a house they could party—or fuck—at, but then Blade slid a hand over his thigh and cupped his balls, and any thought that didn't center around his cock and what he was going to do with it wisped away like smoke.

The limo ride hadn't been long, but between Blade's skillful fingers and the booze still coursing through Jack's system, he was almost ready to strip naked and ride Blade's cock right there in the vehicle, the rest of the passengers be damned.

Their swift arrival at the hotel might have been the only thing that saved his modesty, but Blade tumbled him into a private room with a bed, and Jack didn't have to worry about putting on a public display.

Blade pulled him down on the bed, and Jack wasted no time stripping and attacking the buckles holding Blade's leather vest closed, then shucking off Blade's black leather pants.

The sharp tang of sweat tempered by the earthiness of leather teased his nose, the ultimate masculine scent making Jack's cock throb.

Blade smiled blearily at him, like a sultan waiting for a body servant to pleasure him. Jack didn't know where to start. Tattoos curled around his chest and arms, some of them snaking down his hips and teasing the prominent pelvic bones. His groin had been waxed clean, and Jack shivered. He'd never been with a guy who'd waxed everything away. Blade's heavy cock, ruddy and thick, lay along his hip, a dragon dozing but ready to spring into action at a moment's notice.

Then his gaze fell on the band's logo, tattooed in stark black and red on Blade's defined abs, calling to Jack—the starting point on a treasure map.

He dove for the tattoo and traced it with his tongue, Blade's skin hot and salty. Jack mouthed the taut skin, Blade's erection nudging his chin insistently. He could only ignore the siren song of cock for so long and licked the length. He swirled his tongue around the head and lapped up the pearls of precum slicking the tip.

Blade moaned and shifted restlessly underneath him but didn't do anything to guide the action. Jack could have written a dissertation on that cock, but Blade's balls called louder. He cupped the suede-like scrotum, his tongue teasing the head of Blade's cock. Then he licked his way down and sucked one of those velvet-covered balls into his mouth, wringing another moan, this one breathier and more desperate, from the object of so many fantasies.

Jack moved on to the other testicle, his attention making the skin almost as ruddy as Blade's cock. Then Blade threaded a hand into his hair and tugged, just this side of too hard. Jack let himself be guided and moved up the bed. Blade leered at him, nipped at his lower lip, then reversed their positions so Jack lay under him. Blade sucked at his nipples until they were pouty and red and Jack was barely able to hold still. The smirk Blade gave him was wicked and feral.

The unexpected sensation of slick fingers sliding into him made him yelp. He had no idea when Blade had found the lube, but as soon as he found Jack's gland, it didn't fucking matter. He had never needed to come so bad in his life, and he reached for his dick, desperate to stroke off with Blade's fingers buried inside him.

"Don't."

Jack's eyes flared open. Did Blade truly mean…?

"I mean it. Don't touch your dick." Another wicked smile accompanied the demand, and Jack slid his hands underneath his head, otherwise he wasn't going to be able to obey.

"Touch me. Suck me. Please."

Blade kept stretching his hole, ignoring both his words and his cock. Jack's demands quickly became pleading. He needed to come, he needed to be fucked, and Blade was toying with him. He squirmed and panted and butted up against the edge of orgasm, never tipping over.

"Please, oh God, please fuck me. Fuck me." Was it the booze? Was it his extended dry spell? Was Blade a sex god made flesh? Whatever perfect storm put Jack in this bed, with this man, he didn't know, but the orgasm was going to be epic. Songs would be sung about this moment. Poetry would be written. Jack might never survive.

Out of the corner of his eye, he saw the metallic flash of a condom wrapper. He also didn't know when Blade had managed that part of the operation, but then Jack's only concern right now was his throbbing dick and the fingers inside him, skating over his gland without nearly enough pressure.

Then the fingers were gone and Jack was empty, bereft. Blade shifted, then pushed Jack's knees back, almost to his ears. His cock, slick with precum, waved obscenely between his legs, and his hole was exposed, vulnerable. Blade shifted again, blunt head of his cock seeking entrance.

He rubbed the tip of his cock against Jack's hole, and Jack whimpered deep in his throat. With one swift thrust, Blade pushed home, and Jack howled in ecstasy.

Like Blade could read Jack's mind, he slid his hands up and gripped Jack's wrists, preventing him from reaching down and tugging at himself.

"Please, I have to…." Jack could barely speak.

"No." Blade was implacable, moving his hips harder than seemed possible at his angle. The angle was good for something else, though. Blade's thick erection nosed over Jack's gland with every thrust—endless, beautiful fucking—and he came close to losing his mind.

Then Blade's thrusts sped up, became more forceful, and for a moment, Jack was afraid he'd be left behind, poised on the precipice, mad with lust. Blade shuddered and jerked inside him, then turned his head and bit Jack's calf.

The shock of almost-pain catapulted Jack over the edge, and he spurted wildly, hot, slick spunk landing on his chest, his chin, his lips. His pulse pounded, and he gulped in air, panting like he'd just run a marathon.

Blade sagged limply over him, heavy enough that Jack thought for a moment he'd passed out, but instead he carefully pulled out. Then he did one of the sexiest things Jack had ever experienced. He kissed Jack—the first kiss they'd shared—smearing the drops of

Jack's come against both their lips before sending the flavor deep in Jack's mouth with his tongue.

If it weren't for the epic orgasm mere seconds before, Jack would be hard and raring to go.

Jack dozed briefly in a haze, most of his alcohol buzz burned off by the sex. Sometime later Blade got up to take care of the condom. When he got back to the bed, he smelled, oddly, of fresh alcohol, like he'd had a glass of bourbon in the bathroom.

Perhaps Jack had been asleep longer than he'd thought.

Then Blade smacked him on the ass. "That was great, man." A twenty-dollar bill floated down in front of Jack. "Think that'll be enough for your cab home?"

Jack blinked, wide-awake and stunned as though Blade had doused him in the half-melted ice water in the ice bucket.

"Uh. Yeah, sure."

"Good. Good. I'm gonna take a shower. Maybe we can do it again sometime, Ryan."

Ryan? Blade's words had been somewhat slurred, but not enough to mistake Ryan for Jack.

He stared at Blade's receding naked ass, eyes burning, humiliation setting his cheeks on fire. He'd had one-night stands before and he'd had quickly shared orgasms in club bathrooms, but he'd never once been made to feel so completely… interchangeable. A cheap whore who could be had for the price of cab fare. As though any warm body—Ryan's warm body—would have done.

The alcohol roiled unpleasantly in his stomach, and the second the bathroom door closed behind Blade, he fumbled his clothes back on.

The ghost of Blade's cock haunted his ass for days, a dual reminder of spectacular sex and unparalleled humiliation.

He'd spent too many years as a fan of the band to completely lose his love of the music, but the betrayal—justified or not—had cut deeply. It had taken him a long time to separate the music from the men behind it, but he never quite got over the resentment that Blade had ruined an innocence inside Jack he hadn't even known he'd been nurturing at the grand old age of thirty.

STEPHANIE GAPED at him, and Jack's cheeks flushed, unable to keep the images of that sex out of his mind, even though he certainly wasn't going to share those details with Stephanie.

The server swept back to their table, plunking two excessively garnished Bloody Marys down in the pregnant silence. Jack sucked back a giant mouthful of his drink to irrigate his throat. Had to be a psychosomatic reaction, because he spent hours every day talking at the front of lecture halls.

"I can't believe you slept with him and didn't tell me."

"Uh, did you not hear the last bit? I was humiliated, Steph. It was too fucking embarrassing to talk about."

Stephanie rolled her eyes. "Oh my goodness. The lead singer of a popular band slept with a fan. A fan who was… ahem… well beyond legal age, and who offered it up. I'm shocked. Utterly shocked." She pulled out her phone and waved it around. "I bet we can get this to go viral. Asshole musician has one-night stand."

In spite of his ears joining in the blushing party, she managed to surprise a laugh out of him. "Fine. Fine. But he called me Ryan."

"And he said it was good."

"Not exactly."

"Close enough. You said he was drunk, right? I'd take it as a win."

Drunk, yes. Actually right at the end he'd seemed wasted, too wasted to have been that skilled in bed. Jack had been drunk too, but he'd definitely been sober enough to know the sex had been surface-of-the-sun hot.

He didn't think it would be as easy as Steph seemed to think, shaking off the humiliation he'd internalized for the past four years.

"Oh my God, Jack. That was when you kept making excuses to avoid practice. And why you'd been so damn colorless when we did have gigs. I thought you'd been going through some sort of midlife crisis, but you never would admit anything was wrong. I think I hate you." The effect of her glare was mitigated by her almost poking her eye out with a giant stalk of celery in her drink.

"Wait, what?"

She swallowed heavily. "We've been friends for fucking ever. I told you about my pregnancy scare, and you helped me figure out that ass I'd been sleeping with senior year was a complete creep." They both shuddered. The jerk had taken pictures of her sleeping and kept them in an album with pictures of every other girl he'd ever slept with.

"And?"

"And you should have told me. This friendship is a two-way street, warts, STDs, and all."

Jack let out another laugh. "Well, maybe this will make up for it."

"You mean there's *more*?" Stephanie leaned closer. "Spill. Right now, or I'm never speaking to you again."

"Remember I told you I was covering Intro to Archaeology for a couple of months?"

She waved her hands around. "You did it, didn't you? You slept with that student."

The blood came rushing back to Jack's cheeks. "Shut up, Steph! I did not, but you can't say shit like that." And certainly not that damned loud. He glanced around. No one seemed too interested in their conversation, but baldly stated like that, it made him sound like a fucking pedophile. And relationships with students weren't even against regulations at the university, as long as he informed the appropriate people and didn't put himself in a position to affect grades or access to classes.

"Then what? I mean, aren't Intro students young? I thought you went more for the older guys."

He considered for a mere second about reprimanding her about interruptions, but he decided to rip the bandage right off. "Devlin Waters is in that class."

That one sentence seemed to shock her even more. "What the… you've… why didn't you tell me?" The last word ended on a screech that had most of the neighboring tables glancing their way. Probably thought they were breaking up or something. Stephanie was the only one who'd be guaranteed to know Blade was Devlin Waters's pseudonym with the band, and that included Barry, Kirk, and Ann. They might love the music but never demonstrated much interest in the personal lives of the band members. The exception had been when Reaver had died suddenly and unexpectedly several months ago.

"I am telling you."

"Yeah, two weeks after school started."

"But I only figured it out Friday. And I nearly lost my shit right there in front of the students."

Stephanie's whole demeanor softened, and she got up out of her seat to hug him. "Oh. I see now. I mean, it must have been kind of like the first time you see your ex after getting dumped."

Jack stared at her, the revelation blindingly… revelatory. "Yes. Yes it kind of felt like that. Except it was bigger than that. More like I'd met my first love with their new spouse and they didn't remember me. I don't know why. It's not like he was my boyfriend or anything."

"No, but he was probably your first love. Puppy love. And you held on to that love for a long time, probably built him up into something a mere man could never hope to live up to. And there's no real reason to assume he's not a jerk. A jerk who makes great music."

God. They really didn't know a lot about any of the band members. Very little information was available, and it wasn't like *Rolling Stone* had been chasing them down for interviews, and even recently they hadn't given interviews on blogs or podcasts. "You're right. He was my first love. And disappointment was inevitable."

"So what happened? Did you ask him for his autograph or something? And how come you didn't realize he was in your class? Oh, I know. Friday was the first day he came to class, and you just about passed out when he walked in the room."

He sucked back the last of his drink and signaled the server to get refills for both of them.

"No. Not exactly. He's actually been a bit of a thorn in my side the past two weeks. He's arrogant, and an asshole."

"Uh-huh. Which you'd figured out four years ago."

Jack rolled his eyes. "But I didn't recognize him. Obviously he's not wearing the full makeup job, but… he's…. Shit. He's got freckles.

And his natural hair color is sandy brown. He looks wholesome." And edible, which just wasn't fucking fair.

"No shit? But you slept with him. Surely you knew the carpet didn't match the drapes."

"For God's sake, Steph."

"What? That's the right expression, although I guess they usually save it for redheads, don't they?"

He was going to have to part with one intimate detail. "He was, er, waxed."

She fanned a hand in front of her face. "Oh my sweet baby Jesus, I think I'm gonna die."

"You're a crazy woman. Anyway, I did not take well to the shock. I left in the middle of the lab, hit the bathroom, and seriously considered fainting."

"Yikes. And… wait. Didn't he say something to you? I mean, about, you know. Knocking boots."

"I have to say, it kind of twisted the humiliation factor up a couple of notches. He actually followed me into the bathroom, checking to make sure I was okay." Which was a nice thing to do, however poorly Jack had thanked him for his concern. "He truly doesn't remember me. At all. And aside from not wearing unrelieved black, I don't look any different than I did at thirty."

"Oh. Yeah, that sucks big-time. Maybe you should tell him your real name is Ryan."

Stephanie made it very hard to hold on to a bad mood. "Uh, I don't think so. But I'm having a hard time staying objective."

"Cuz you want to bone the boy-next-door version, see if it's different."

"That's part of the problem. He's infuriating and attractive all at the same time, and then I realize he's actually someone I dislike." Or even sort of hated for the past four years, and one moment of humanity couldn't erase the Mount Kilimanjaro–level assholery. "I'm not sure what to do."

"Surely you've taught douchebags before."

"Yeah, but they weren't douchebags I'd slept with!"

Stephanie shrugged. “It’s not even really your class. Until you can ditch it, get someone else to mark his stuff, if you truly think you can’t be objective. Other than that, treat him as any other douchenozzle you’ve taught. Because I know you. Even if you’re going to sleep with him again, it won’t be until you’re done with this class.”

And assuming Devlin didn’t decide to take up any of his other classes. But he didn’t expect Devlin to have the fortitude to stick it out in this one class, never mind staying long enough to come back next year. What did a wealthy musician need with archaeology classes, for fuck’s sake?

He sighed. “Yeah, I think you’re right. That’s what I’ll do.” Probably he could escape without documenting his stupidity, as long as he got Sanji or Meredith to grade any tests or activities.

“I will, of course, expect regular updates. And as soon as you get the balls to tell him you know about the fucking band, I’d better get an introduction. Make it soon, or I’m crashing your class.”

Jack was saved from figuring out how to reply to that by the arrival of Stephanie’s husband.

“Good morning,” Ian boomed out before kissing his wife. The server returned with two more Bloody Marys, and Ian chuckled. “I see you started without me.”

Stephanie scoffed. “Please. This is already our second. You are well behind.”

Ian sat down between them and looked earnestly at Jack. “How are things? Classes going well?”

Jack shrugged while Stephanie smothered an evil laugh. “Oh, a few ups and downs.”

The conversation moved into safer territory, and Jack took the reprieve. There would be plenty of time to stress about facing Devlin first thing Monday morning.

CHAPTER FIVE

DEVLIN WAS early. He didn't expect Jack to give him any props for that, but commendable nonetheless. He'd spent the weekend reading, studying, and beginning papers. He'd forgotten how much he enjoyed classes; it had all been superseded by the growing success of Negative Impression, and then, it hadn't occurred to him to miss it, not even when his dad had worked it into conversation, however awkwardly.

Most importantly, he had questions for Jack and a few… less scholarly questions for Jack's office hours later in the day. He'd be skipping a psychology class for that, but he was thinking about dropping that one anyway. It didn't fulfill any requirement he didn't already have, and it bored him senseless. He just hoped Jack had truly been ill Friday, and not only because tweaking Jack's nose had quickly become his favorite activity of his new university life.

The lecture hall filled in around him, and multiple conversations raised the decibel level. Debbie, his lab partner from Friday, walked in with a couple of her friends, and she waved at him before making her way to the back of the room. Another guy he recognized from his lab sat beside him.

"Hey, man."

Devlin blinked. "Uh. Hey."

"I'm Ken."

"Hi, Ken. I'm Devlin. Nice to meet you."

"You too."

That seemed to be the end of their conversation, but it made Devlin smile. He couldn't tell if Ken was happy to see a vaguely familiar face or if he thought Devlin would make a useful study partner or if he wanted in Devlin's pants. He wasn't a cradle robber, but Devlin wouldn't mind either of the other options.

Jack chose that moment to walk in, wrinkling his nose ever so slightly and drawing all of Devlin's attention. What Dev wouldn't give to dress that man in skintight black and slap some eyeliner on him. Dev shivered, just imagining it. Absolutely fucking wasted in chinos and a preppy button-down shirt.

Then that icy blue gaze landed on Dev, and he returned it with an unconcerned smile. Pink flashed into those pale cheeks, and Jack's gaze danced away.

What did he do with all that pale skin when he was on digs in equatorial regions? Zinc oxide from head to toe?

He tilted his head. Maybe jungles had enough shade to keep Dr. Jack from spontaneously combusting. He'd have to put that question in his back pocket for later. It was perfectly legitimate, and it would irritate Jack to have to answer it. Perfect. But really, why wait?

Dev raised his hand and waved it. He was close enough to hear Jack sigh. "Yes?" Why Dev got a kick out of that exasperated tone, he wasn't quite sure.

"Don't you burn when you're doing fieldwork?"

Jack's nostrils flared in annoyance. "Irrelevant to today's discussion." He shuffled his notes and started the lecture.

Amateur. Like that was going to stop Dev. Office hours were only a couple of hours away. He slouched in his chair and spread his legs. At some point Dr. Jack's gaze was going to slide right across his crotch, and it would fluster him for just a split second. His quick recovery had Devlin wondering if his gaydar was on the fritz or not, but he had more information today. Jack was into men and was not in the closet. His mother might not have had this in mind when she'd told him to make some new friends. Ken or Debbie were more in line with her thinking, but Devlin had fixated on his professor—hot, stern, smart, and had passion for a field of study Dev also found interesting.

Friends. With benefits. Or maybe even more, but there wasn't much point in considering that until he'd figured out if the prickly exterior hid a soft marshmallow center or not. Or if the prickly exterior was interested in dating someone seriously. His new information suggested Dr. Jack didn't have a boyfriend or husband, but he'd have to confirm that as well. His mother would absolutely murder him if he attempted to weasel his way into an established relationship. He was lucky she didn't know about that one time… he'd been a complete fucking asshole. For reasons, to be sure, but that wouldn't have mitigated anything if his mother had found out.

He spent some time picturing Dr. Jack naked in his bed, maybe giving orders in that haughty tone of his. Goddamn, but that would be something. Dev wasn't much on taking orders, but something about Jack made him think it might be fun. He'd spent the better part of his life as a professional rebel. Maybe a little compliance was in the cards. Unless Jack liked submitting in private, after wrangling obnoxious students—like Dev—five days a week.

Dev caught Jack's gaze once more and licked his lips suggestively. Jack couldn't quite suppress a shiver, and Dev couldn't hold back a smug smile. Hell, he wouldn't much care how they did it, as long as they got naked together eventually.

It had been a long time since he'd had so much fun. And he'd never had the chance for a long-term flirtation like this.

Then Jack assigned the required reading, and Dev sat up straight. Shit. He'd managed to not only miss the entire lecture but failed to ask any questions. He knew his fellow students didn't find Jack's lectures interesting, and that was something he wanted to ask Jack about, although not in the class, and maybe not even at today's office hours. That might be too ballsy, even for him.

Jack scampered away, dodging any after-class questions, and Devlin sighed. Even in less-than-snug professor garb, there was no hiding Jack's world-class ass. He pulled out his phone. More emails from Luke and Mo he could delete.

"So, uh, Devlin?" He shifted his focus to Ken, who was a cute Asian kid, but like all the classmates he'd told his mom about, young enough to be his own kid.

"Yeah, Ken?" He prayed Ken wasn't going to ask him out, although he hadn't got any pings on his gaydar for this one.

"I'm doing a membership drive for my social club. I was hoping you might stop by and check it out."

Social club? What the ever-loving fuck was that? Was that what students were calling dating these days? He hadn't done much to keep up on slang, but even he had to admit that sounded dorky as hell.

"Um. I'll think about it."

Ken frowned at him. "Don't you want to know about it?"

Not really. But he could also hear his mom scolding him, and he sighed. "Sure thing."

"Great. Can I see your phone?"

Devlin gritted his teeth and handed it over. He'd gone to such lengths while on tour to avoid giving out any sort of personal contact information, but it had taken him all of a day in university to realize that brand of privacy didn't fly with these kids.

"Okay. I've got your number; you've got mine. I'll text you with details. We meet twice a week."

"Whoa. I thought you were going to tell me about it?" Surely something like "we socialize and make small talk" would take about thirty seconds, and they could do that right here. Dev could say he'll think about it and then make excuses for the rest of the school year. He was pretty sure he'd never committed to attending.

"I'll take you to dinner first, give you the overview, then, if it sounds good, I can show up with you and introduce you, so you don't have to walk into a room full of strangers."

Dev squinted at Ken. This almost sounded like some sort of hazing prank for pledging a fraternity, but Dev's previous experience with university had shown him the whole "Greek" culture wasn't much of a thing, at least at this university, or presumably other Canadian universities. The frats and sororities were around, but it wasn't like it was in the movies.

Also, Ken looked sincere as shit, and Negative Impression hadn't gotten successful because its members played it safe.

"Fine. We'll make a plan. But no promises to attend." Even though his future plans included nothing but class, homework, and the occasional meal with his mom. She'd be cat-ate-the-canary smug to find out he'd been invited to join a social club. He frowned.

Ken nodded and grinned. "No promises."

Devlin tucked his phone away, grabbed his bag, and headed for his next class.

JACK TRIED to get some work done, but every time someone walked past his office, he flinched. For whatever reason, Devlin hadn't asked nearly as many questions as he had the previous week, but that hadn't been the reprieve Jack had expected. Knowing he'd slept with Devlin, knowing Devlin couldn't recall him from any other damned man he'd fucked, had only made Jack hyperaware of Devlin in a way he hadn't been before. Every fiery look, every rumbled word, every indolent move. Everything about Devlin grabbed his attention while he desperately tried to keep Devlin from realizing that, and it made him jumpy as hell.

Devlin hadn't cornered him at office hours before, and if he thought about it with a clear head, actively seeking him out didn't make sense. Devlin had to be just fucking with him because he could, because of their proximity. Probably he gave all of his professors shit because he was an accomplished musician, with a successful band; his arrogance was well earned, dammit.

His phone buzzed, and he jumped. As he'd discussed with Stephanie, he should just be able to let it go, but maybe it would take some time. And sure as shit, he shouldn't be giving a one-night stand—however many years he'd been crushing on the man—so much power over his mental state.

Snatching up his phone, he checked his messages. Matt. Wanting another date. He let out a breath in a little puff of pleasure. Not that he thought Matt was the one, but he seemed nice, and he hadn't been in a properly receptive mood on Friday.

He fired off a reply before he could consider if he was supposed to wait some prescribed period of time before responding. Screw it. He didn't have all that much free time that he wanted to squander it in game playing.

Maybe Matt would seem more exciting when he hadn't been all bamboozled by his revelation about Devlin Waters.

"Dr. Jack" came the greeting from the door. Jack managed—barely—to keep his head from thunking down on his desk. He wasn't a believer in old-school folklore about the power of names, although he'd enjoyed its application as "he who shall not be named" in *Harry Potter*, but here Devlin was, as though the mere thought of his name had conjured the man up.

"Good afternoon. What can I do for you, Devlin?" He nearly choked on that name. When he'd had sex with Devlin, he'd called him Blade. For all that Blade was the pseudonym, he'd spent years thinking of the man as Blade. Calling him Devlin, seeing him in this sepia-toned alter ego was a bit of a mind fuck.

Devlin smirked at him. Without an invitation from Jack, he threw himself in the chair across from Jack's desk.

In the close confines of Jack's office, the faint musk of Devlin's cologne became more pervasive. He didn't think it was the same one he'd worn that fateful day four years ago, but more than likely sweat and leather had overpowered it.

That didn't mean Jack didn't want to stick his nose in Devlin's neck and sniff and lick… and hate himself for being a weak-willed doormat.

"I had a few questions."

"Not that sunscreen question?" He'd not slept well all weekend, and his patience had officially run out. "What are you really doing here, Devlin? Why are you even bothering with this whole university thing—terminal boredom?" His tone was sharp and spiky, like his mood, with a contemptuous undercurrent.

But he hadn't expected Devlin's eyes to widen. He hadn't expected to see pain, deep and searing, in those hazel eyes. Hadn't believed anything could pierce that placid, imperious carapace.

Even if he thought he could hurt, he hadn't meant to, and his tone was out of line for any student, even one who tried his patience. Before Jack could formulate a reply, Devlin launched out of the chair and was gone.

Jack sucked in a shocked breath, then scrambled around his desk. Whatever past they'd had—and it was one night, that only Jack remembered—this wasn't who he was.

He bounded out the door, Devlin was much farther down the hall than Jack would have expected, even though he wasn't actually running.

"Devlin, wait," Jack called out, but Devlin didn't slow. "Devlin, dammit! Come back here."

Devlin came to a stop but didn't turn around, just shifted back and forth, like he was waiting for a starter's pistol and then he'd be off again.

Jack hustled down the hall and drew up beside Devlin. "I'm sorry. I'm so sorry. I was way out of line."

Devlin wouldn't look him in the eye, and the pinched look of his lips told Jack he hadn't made things right. Dammit, Stephanie was right. He'd somehow forgotten that Devlin was a human being, an imperfect human with feelings. Not some automaton who sang songs for Jack's pleasure. Jury was still out on whether he was a giant dick of imperfect human, but that didn't mean he was devoid of emotion.

He laid a gentle hand on Devlin's arm. "Come back to my office. Please. I… I've been under some stress, and I took it out on you."

Devlin didn't reply but turned around and followed Jack back down the hall. Jack didn't look back, afraid he'd see a defeated slump rather than the cocky insouciance he'd come to expect from Devlin and which suited him better than anything else.

Back in Jack's office, they returned to their seats, but the memory of Jack's words hung there, jangling Jack's nerves worse than Devlin normally did. They revealed how harmless Devlin's attitude was in comparison. If not for their sort-of-shared naked history, Jack wouldn't have reacted nearly so badly to Devlin. Probably. But that didn't change the fact that Jack's office could use a good airing out.

He stared at Devlin's profile, because the man still wouldn't meet his gaze. Freckles. Golden skin. A glint of red in the stubble that lined his jaw. Crinkles beside his eyes. This was the man under the makeup, and it suited him more than Jack could have ever imagined. He sighed.

"You ever had the fries from the food truck outside the library?"

That caught Devlin's attention, and he turned a confused expression on Jack, who manfully swallowed a grin.

"No." Devlin tilted his head to the side and examined Jack in a dispassionate manner.

"Let's go grab some. I missed lunch, and they're fantastic. It's just a short walk." He'd be a total write-off for any other student right now anyway.

Devlin stared at him, the silence lengthening.

"My treat." Jack was getting desperate.

"Fine. Let's see if they live up to the hype."

Jack snorted. "You'll see."

AFTER JACK locked up his office, they walked the four blocks to the food truck in mostly companionable silence. Jack hoped it was companionable. Devlin had lost that tense, defensive set to his shoulders at least.

Jack bought two orders of fries, thick, salty wedges of potatoes that were fresh out of the fryer, and handed one to Devlin. There wasn't much in the way of seating, so they sat on a concrete ledge surrounding a profusion of evergreen shrubbery.

The late-afternoon sun was warm on their faces but, as it was already almost the end of September, not overheating.

Devlin poked a finger into his fries and snatched it back. "Shit. They're hot."

"Yup. I'd wait a minute or two before trying to eat them." Already, the atmosphere had eased. Jack didn't know if it was the different venue or the application of salty potato goodness, but he wasn't going to complain.

"I really am sorry for snapping at you."

Devlin lifted a shoulder. "I get it. I can be annoying. It's a gift."

Jack laughed. "Or a talent."

"True."

"I expressed myself very poorly, but I really am curious. What brings you to the university?" Office hours were supposed to be for the benefit of the students, but Jack's desire to know had become almost unbearable.

For a moment it seemed as though Devlin hadn't heard him or didn't plan to answer. Then he huffed out a sigh. "I guess you could say I'm at a proverbial crossroads in my life. I'm currently unemployed, I'm too young to retire, and I'm trying to please my dad, who was always ticked off that I dropped out of school before I got my degree."

Unemployed? Jack knew Reaver, the other founding member of Negative Impression, died earlier in the year, but he hadn't heard anything about Devlin leaving the band. The band was on hiatus, obviously. One didn't just replace a person like they were a used-up battery, so that didn't make Devlin unemployed. But he wasn't sure he wanted to pry. Nor did he want to admit he knew exactly who Devlin was. Devlin might not be hiding, not quite, but he certainly wasn't advertising his identity as Blade.

"You dropped out? Did you complete any courses?"

"Yeah. Got the required first-year courses before I… jumped into a career that didn't need a degree."

Definitely not advertising Negative Impression. Jack would have to be careful nothing slipped.

"So what are you doing taking more first-year courses? Shouldn't you be focusing on courses for a major?"

Devlin let out a wry laugh and stuffed a fry into his mouth. Then quickly huffed air and waved a hand in front of his face. "Hot." Potato muffled the word.

Jack grinned. "Told ya. But good, right?"

A few seconds later, Devlin shut his mouth and chewed, eyes closing in bliss. "Mmm." He swallowed. "Those are great fries. Thank you."

They both ate a few fries, then Devlin picked up the conversation where they'd left it. "So, I did the requirements. And they were fine. But it was like, twenty years ago. More, even. Nothing grabbed my attention, so right now I'm taking a bunch of first-year courses, um, auditioning for a second career, I suppose."

A second career? What the fuck would he need that for? Just because he left the band didn't mean he wasn't still a musician. Surely he could just move on to some other sort of band or music or even teaching music.

This new knowledge was almost more irritating, because it made Devlin intriguing, and Jack didn't need to care about Devlin's life.

"A second career. That's a pretty common reason to come back to school." He bit back a question about whether Devlin had found anything that piqued his interest yet—partly because they weren't even three full weeks into the semester and partly because he didn't know if he wanted Devlin to be interested in archaeology or not. It would be another severe blow to his ego if Devlin found it boring, even though Jack had been deliberately trying to drive out the dabblers and glory seekers with sheer ennui.

Jack ate a few more fries as he considered his next words. "If you have any questions, I'll be happy to answer them. Even about other disciplines. I mean, I might not know the answers, but if nothing else, I can point you in the right direction."

He might be setting himself up for more irritation, but he wasn't ready to wash his hands of Devlin Waters. Not until he got answers to some of his own questions.

"Thanks. I might take you up on it." Devlin paused to eat more, then set the fries down beside him before popping up and jogging the few steps to the food truck. He returned bearing two cans of cola, condensation making the red aluminum glitter.

He offered one to Jack with a jaunty little bow. "My treat." If not for their little chat, Jack might have assumed Devlin was mocking him. And he was, just a bit, but Jack could see it now as teasing.

Jack might not ever forgive Devlin for that one humiliating night, but he might be able to finally admit that Devlin had redeeming qualities beyond his musical ability.

"Thank you. Perfect choice to go with fries." Jack was uncomfortably reminded of his date with Matt and his wine snobbery.

After Devlin settled back beside him, he cleared his throat. "I wasn't actually trying to piss you off when I asked about your skin. Seriously, you must burn like a vampire on tetracycline. I was curious. I mean… I've traveled all over the world, but I know nothing about archaeology aside from movies."

Jack paused for a moment, wondering if he should comment on the "all over the world" bit but in the end decided not to.

"I guess I just… misjudged your sincerity." Jack grinned ruefully. "Lecture halls don't see too many hecklers, but they show up occasionally."

Devlin laughed hard enough he snorted. Jack found himself charmed, which perversely annoyed him further. Devlin wasn't supposed to be charming, but it never occurred to him to wonder if Devlin ever laughed or what he sounded like when he did. A sense of humor was something else a good little band member didn't need, not until Jack needed to start accepting Devlin's humanity. It was a good laugh. Strong and infectious.

"An archaeology heckler. That's a good one. Seriously, though… I find the lessons interesting. But I might be the only one. I've heard a lot of grumbles about dropping out. Uh… not to criticize or anything but… you clearly love your field of study. Isn't there some way to, I don't know, bump up the entertainment value?"

Jack's nostrils flared. "Entertainment? No one is here to be *entertained*."

Devlin sent an eyebrow toward his hairline. "Whoa. Okay, wrong word. Maybe just changing up the order of lectures? The syllabus mentions some topics that might have more universal appeal."

He was a fucking idiot. Of course Devlin would think in terms of appeal and entertainment; his career—up until now—relied on packed venues and ticket sales. A far cry from the delicate balance professors aimed for: enough demand for their classes to keep their jobs but teaching the absolute minimum of students once that threshold had been reached.

Maybe not all professors aimed for that goal, but he sure did.

"And that day you talked about your field of study—that was awesome. I know I wasn't the only one who thought so."

Jack couldn't help but preen a little, even though it shouldn't matter if Devlin approved or paid attention.

"I'll let you in on a little secret." Jack looked around, as though checking for spies. "I'm doing that on purpose," he stage-whispered.

While Devlin blinked in shock, Jack stuffed the last of his fries in his mouth and washed them down with the sugary drink that somehow tasted better for Devlin having bought it for him.

"On purpose? I don't understand."

"Here's the thing. Archaeology really isn't what people see in the movies. If that's what they want, they should be taking up film studies or cinematography. Not archaeology. Which means, for those students, it's not only a waste of their time, and my time, but a waste of their money if they don't drop out early enough. You do know there are over four hundred students in your class, right?"

Devlin shrugged. "Seemed a bit less than that to me, but close, sure."

Interesting. Jack hadn't thought about it before, but it made sense that someone who played in front of live audiences for a living might develop a good sense of how many people were in that audience at just a glance.

Instead of commenting on that, Jack gave Devlin a look. "The class is at nine on Monday morning. Not everyone shows."

"Touché. It's tough."

"Anyway, we have a rough idea how many students are going to make it all the way through the year, and of those, approximately how many will pass. Until those kids drop out, though, we still have to conduct tests and grade papers and mark practical exercises. Now I'm just filling in for Professor Nadine Redmond, but my personal philosophy when I get stuck teaching Intro is to, well, bore them into dropping out earlier than they might otherwise. The date for dropping out and getting a refund is quite early, but they have until February to drop out without academic penalty. We try to get most everyone out before the financial deadline, and then it's just steady attrition until February."

Devlin stared at Jack as though he were one of those bug-eyed space aliens, then he started laughing again, that disgustingly engaging snort-laugh that could be nothing but genuine.

"You do it *on purpose*. I can't… I can't even…." He sucked in a few breaths between laughing. "Oh my fucking God, you should hear some of the things they say."

Well, that explained the laughter. "Uh, no. Probably better that I don't know."

Devlin shook his head. "Nah. I mean, it's not too awful, and I've never agreed, but knowing you're being boring on purpose and the kids don't know that—fucking hilarious."

They sat there for a few more minutes, but with the fries gone, and the air cleared, Jack didn't know what else to say that wouldn't be prying. Stephanie wouldn't hold back, and maybe if Jack wasn't the professor, he might not have either.

Then again, Jack's careless words and hurtful tone had created genuine pain earlier. Jack didn't know what caused it, and he wasn't sure this was the right time, nor if he was the right person to delve into that. He functioned as an advisor to grad students, and although that sometimes strayed into the realm of dealing with stress or money or family, his primary role was to counsel students on academic-related issues. This was out of his comfort zone.

"I'd better get going." Devlin stood as he made the announcement, beating Jack to the punch.

"Me too. I've got a lot of work to do."

Devlin's lips curled into a tiny half smile, bordering on a smirk, but Jack might just be reading into that. Then again, there was no reason to assume Devlin's humor wasn't sardonic or sarcastic. It might not have the meanings Jack had imbued based on that one night where Jack ended up—legitimately or otherwise—feeling utterly betrayed. Jack didn't really know anything about Devlin, not at all, and he needed to not make judgments based on a few hours of drunken sex and years of being a fanboy.

"See you in class Wednesday."

Jack nodded and couldn't stop himself from adding, "Don't forget my office hours."

"I won't. I'll make use of 'em if I need to."

Devlin slung his bag over his shoulder and sauntered away. Everything about the guy screamed sex, and Jack didn't know if it was natural grace or charm practiced over years of being at the center of attention, but Jack was as susceptible as ever. Not that he could ever admit it.

He wished it was appropriate to request Devlin wear looser clothes, if only so he could properly concentrate on his lectures. It took effort to stay on the dullest topics and not get sucked into more interesting tangents.

DEVLIN SLUMPED in his chair at his mom's kitchen table. She hadn't cooked today but had stopped by Mr. Sub to pick up one of Devlin's favorites—a tuna sub with extra pickles and extra mayo. She'd gotten a pizza sub, and she grinned at him with slightly orange-tinged lips, at odds with her tailored navy skirt and pale pink blouse. His mother had the miraculous ability to avoid getting tomato sauce on her clothes, an ability that Devlin both admired and envied.

For all that he had plenty of money, when touring, his diet had consisted of mostly crap, including subs although he loved coming home to things like Mr. Sub, and burgers from Harvey's, and butter tarts, and nanaimo bars that he couldn't get anywhere else. His mother, though, rarely indulged, and it made him happy to see her enjoying herself.

It gave him hope that one day he'd be on the other side of this. Trent hadn't been his spouse, hadn't been his boyfriend, hadn't been his lover. Devlin hadn't been in love with his best friend, but they'd both been only children who'd grown up together. Trent had been the brother of his heart, and every day meant waking up and moving his feet even though he had this invisible gaping wound threatening to level him. The best he could do was wrap it up tightly and try to pretend it wasn't there.

Most times, Jack's classes and the man himself made him feel alive again. Teasing Jack, however subtly, made him feel normal. Today had been hard. Jack hadn't meant to do it, but he'd made Devlin peek under the bandages, just for a moment, and it had shaken him. Because there was another, older bandage covering a wound that hadn't quite healed as well as he'd thought. He wanted to ask his mom how she did it, how she'd moved on. Because she'd loved his dad; that hadn't been a lie or a façade, and she'd been devastated.

"Been a while since we've had subs together." His mom definitely had a sixth sense about when he needed a pick-me-up.

"Yeah. Just what I needed today, thanks." Fortunately his trip home on the GO Train had allowed him to wrap his feelings back up, get himself more or less pulled together, even if his bandages were nothing more than duct tape and bubble gum, and getting more fragile by the day.

Jack had seemed to know fries would help earlier; he must have a similar talent to Dev's mother.

"How did it go today?"

Devlin shrugged. "Okay. I… had someone invite me to a social club." Telling his mother about almost losing his shit in a professor's office wasn't in the cards. A simple unexpected reminder about his loss could crack his defenses, which was precisely why he couldn't talk to Luke or Mo. They wouldn't just crack his defenses; it would be a full-scale attack, and he wasn't ready.

At least this one truth made his mom smile. "That's great, kid. What does one do at a social club these days?"

"I don't know, but I think it's more complicated than just socializing."

His mother raised an eyebrow. "Really?"

Devlin shrugged. "All I know is that I need a preparatory session, to explain how it works, and then if I'm still interested, I'll get introduced to the group."

She wrinkled her nose. "That sounds odd, doesn't it? You don't suppose it's one of those secret societies, the ones that want you to commit felonies and whatnot to help a fellow member out?"

Devlin laughed—the third time in a single day. It had been a long time, and he hadn't realized he was still capable of laughter until Jack had shown him otherwise. Maybe laughing, like living, was just like riding a bike. Just had to keep at it, and muscle memory would kick in until it was real.

"What exactly have you been watching on television? Because that sounds like the plot to… a number of bad movies I've watched."

His mother blushed. "Just be careful, okay? You're still my baby."

That was worthy of an eye roll. "Thanks, Mom. But you know, I managed touring all over the world for years with what was essentially a punk band and came away without even one stint in rehab."

None of them had, and Devlin had been eternally thankful that the rest of the band members had been as levelheaded as he and Trent had been. They hadn't bought into the whole straight edge movement—it had some laudable concepts, considering the reputation the punk scene in general had with respect to drugs, but went too far the opposite way in many cases. Negative Impression had been drug-free, and although they drank alcohol, they sort of policed themselves, keeping an eye out for behaviors that indicated problems. There hadn't been any, thankfully, and the four of them had become a little family out there on the road.

"I know, I know. Your father and I were always very proud of how you conducted yourselves." She opened her mouth, and Devlin knew what she wanted to say, since he'd been the one to give her the opening. He gave her a hard look, and she subsided.

"Anyway, Ken doesn't look like any sort of secret society member."

His mom smirked. "That's the whole point, isn't it? Stay under the radar."

He wasn't going to hear the end of this. She'd already accepted the idea of secret societies as the work of fiction and utterly ridiculous, but he now saw she was amused by the idea.

"And who is Ken? Is he cute?"

That was worthy of another eye roll. "Young enough I could be his father, remember?" Jack wasn't. Jack was a few years younger but not cradle-robbing young. He smiled. He might even have tacit permission to tease.

"If you think he's cute and he's not underage… I'd like to see you settle down, and that smile tells me you like him."

Nope, that smile was for Jack, not Ken, but he didn't need his mother butting into his love life. He definitely wasn't ready for anything serious, no matter how enticing that ass under chinos was. He'd need to be more careful.

"You're mistaken. He's not gay, and I'm not looking." At Ken.

"I'd like you to give that social club a try. For me." Her expression became serious. "If you aren't ready to talk to Luke and Mo, please, please find someone else."

"Didn't you want me to just get off the couch and out of the house a few weeks ago?"

No mistaking her smug air. "And look how well that worked out."

"Sure, Mom." Devlin was pretty sure he'd attend the social club at least once, just to appease his mother. She'd been worried about him, and he didn't want that.

They moved on to less volatile topics of conversation, mostly centered on her upcoming fund-raisers and Devlin's classes, although he carefully edited anything he told her about archaeology and its delicious professor.

BACK IN his house, he flopped on the bed and stared at the pile of books on the desk. He'd read ahead in all of his classes, some more than most, and he'd already started on all of his assigned papers. Simple interest accounted for most of it, but back before the band had any solid management, Devlin had been the one to file paperwork, set up gigs, meet deadlines. Just his way. He didn't even like being late, unless it served another purpose, like making a point or making a dramatic entrance.

Instead, he grabbed his laptop and searched for "social clubs" on the university's website. Maybe he could find out more about this so-called social club.

Holy fuck. Devlin stared at the page and clicked through a few more pages of results. Hundreds of clubs. Some of the titles were super specific, to the point Devlin couldn't imagine they had more than a handful of participants, but some were so broadly generic.... Devlin didn't even know where to start.

Maybe his mom hadn't been too far off. How hard could it be to bury some innocuous-seeming group into this sea of options, covering any world domination schemes in covert language? Hell, they could probably stick the term Illuminati right there in the description and most people would probably think they were doing cosplay or something.

He shook himself. Now he was getting fanciful. Probably it would be something terrible like… recreating the marriage marts of England's Regency, or cosplaying the War of 1812, or… shit. What about furries? He was pretty sure that was the term for people who liked to dress up in animal costumes before having sex… during sex? He didn't know, but some sort of fetish club that was outside the standard BDSM stuff might explain why Ken felt it needed an introduction and explanation.

BDSM wasn't really his thing aside from the occasional bondage or role-play in the bedroom, despite spending years wearing mostly black leather. Over time he'd met a number of people in the life; he could hang out at a BDSM social club, but that didn't keep Devlin from worrying Ken had something else in mind.

Although he wasn't going to do a general Google search for terms specific to furries—that was asking for trouble—Devlin did another quick search on the university site checking for the keywords furries and animals, but nothing terrifying came back. He did find a club that seemed to revolve around fund-raising for environmental and endangered species charities and bookmarked that. That might be more his thing, if Ken's club didn't work out.

Then he started checking out ones that related to archaeology. There were no obvious indications that the groups required faculty sponsors, or even if faculty was welcomed, but he bookmarked the archaeology ones too. Just in case.

His phone buzzed with a text. Ken.

Club meets @ 7 wed & fri. Wed no good dinner after arch lab fri?

Devlin sighed. At least he assumed the pizza icon meant dinner. Was this what he had to look forward to if he started dating someone in the digital age? Maybe someone closer to his age would use capitals and punctuation. He had a feeling Dr. Jack texted with proper spelling and grammar as well. Devlin didn't mind casual or anything, but Ken's text bordered on indecipherable.

Waiting until Friday to find out what he'd gotten himself into sucked, but he'd promised his mom. His social calendar gaped wide open until the end of time; he certainly didn't have anything better to do.

Friday sounds good.

He was extra careful to capitalize and punctuate, not that Ken would notice or care. He skimmed his emails, ignoring another two emails from Luke, and then he turned off his phone, flung it on the desk, and fired up *Raiders of the Lost Ark*. After making himself comfortable in the nest of pillows on his bed, he spent the whole movie imagining Jack running through the jungle like Indiana Jones.

Sometime during *Temple of Doom*, he fell asleep, and dreamed of defeating giant grave-robbing chipmunks with Dr. Jack at his side.

CHAPTER SIX

"SO WE'RE all on the same page for this exercise?" Jack asked his two TAs in the weekly meeting they had to prepare for the lab sessions. The first exercise was a freebie—no one in the department wanted to put effort into grading shit before the financial drop deadline—but this week's counted.

They both nodded. Each of them was responsible for grading the people in their labs and it was important that all three of them graded consistently. This wasn't like calculus or anatomy or something. Archaeology didn't always have definitive answers, although the first few exercises lowballed the difficulty and dialed up the tedium. Potsherds. It took a special soul to understand what potsherds could say about the people who'd fired and used the vessel.

"Right. Any questions?"

Meredith and Sanji shook their heads.

"Good. Then that's it for now." They both stood, probably planning to grab an early lunch before plunging into the afternoon's lab sessions.

Jack bit his lip, not sure if he needed to do this or not. Yesterday, at Wednesday's class, Devlin hadn't distracted him. Not with questions, at any rate. Those heated, flirtatious looks and form-fitting jeans? Those had still been distracting, especially since he didn't have as much irritation to temper it. At least he'd be able to hold strong against any invitations to have sex. He'd been there, been done, and been dismissed. However attractive Devlin's attentions were, Jack knew all too well he never wanted to repeat that experience. Or at least, didn't want to repeat the postsex humiliation aftershow.

Then Devlin had showed up at his office hours, smelling awesome and armed with all the questions he'd not asked in class, as well as several about his other classes. More specifically, questions related to the careers that could be built using those disciplines as a base. Jack hadn't been able to speak much to psychology, aside from the basic therapist/researcher/teacher, but he was more familiar with history and definitely with anthropology.

After all, anthropology, especially physical anthropology, had a number of parallels with archaeology. They'd avoided any emotional topics, ended up with more of a conversation Jack would expect from a peer or someone he was dating rather than a typical student/professor exchange. When another student showed up at his door, Devlin had swiftly and politely excused himself, leaving Jack partially aroused and disappointed they hadn't been able to talk longer.

"Sanji, can you stay back a moment?" No more waffling. His emotions around Devlin were still too volatile; this had to be done.

"Of course." Meredith gave them both a quick smile and continued on out of the office.

Sanji sat down again and waited. Jack sighed.

"I need to ask you a favor."

"Sure." He nodded to emphasize his willingness.

"Remember I mentioned a Devlin Waters last week?"

"He asked you out? Took him long enough."

Shock froze Jack's words in his throat as he stared at Sanji, who winked. Jack coughed, breaking the paralysis on his vocal cords.

"No. Why would you ask that?"

"Even I can see he's hot. And with the same name as the guy in that band you like and the way he looks at you, well I figured it was only a matter of time."

The skin Devlin had likened to vampiric flashed nearly hot enough to raise the temperature in the room. The last thing he needed was the entire student body gossiping about him.

"I'm not going to date him. Or… or… anything else. Is it all so obvious? Is everyone talking about it? Or reporting it?" His voice cracked. This was worse than he'd thought.

Sanji's teasing expression fell away. "Calm down, please. No one's reporting anything. I'm the only one who knows you well enough to see that he gets to you. I mean, half of those students stare at you like they're imagining you naked, and it's like you never even notice."

What? He didn't think it was possible to die from embarrassment, but he just might want to. "They do no such thing."

"Oh sure. Do you know how many requests both Meredith and I have gotten from students wanting to attend your lab sessions? I can't even imagine the collective disappointment when Nadine takes this class back."

"You're being ridiculous."

Sanji chuckled. "No wonder it doesn't faze you. You really don't notice them."

"Oh my God, stop. You're killing me. How am I supposed to teach the cretins now?"

That only made Sanji laugh more. "Anyway, I knew something was up when he managed to get you to deviate from the syllabus, and it made me pay more attention. You mentioning him last week only confirmed I was right."

Jack gaped at him, and Sanji hurried to reassure him. "Seriously, I'm the only one who'd notice."

Jack let his shoulders slump. "Nothing's happened." Recently. "Nothing is going to happen."

Sanji frowned, as though he was hoping Jack would throw himself at a student. Maybe his dry spell made him grouchier than he realized. He had a second date with Matt tomorrow. Too soon for him to get laid, but hopefully they were laying the groundwork for eventual sex.

"Then what's the matter?"

"You have to keep this confidential, okay? I don't want to be responsible for this information getting out." Assuming anyone would care. Even if Jack posted flyers announcing Devlin's identity, his class wasn't going to get mobbed, and most of his fellow students were probably too young to have even heard of Negative Impression, with a few pierced, tattooed, black-clad exceptions. The most important part of this consideration, though, was the fact that Devlin had made no mention of his band at all, which told Jack he was doing his best to be incognito, even if he wasn't actively hiding.

Maybe Devlin wouldn't care if people knew, but Jack couldn't be the one to make that decision. He was only breaking his silence now to avoid having to fill out paperwork, and he couldn't guarantee who'd see that or who they'd tell about it. Honestly, as long as he kept them at arm's length, official paperwork would be officially overkill.

"Absolutely. You can trust me."

"So, I found out at last week's lab that our Devlin Waters is in fact *the* Devlin Waters, also known as Blade from Negative Impression."

"No shit? That's cool. I guess he used to dye his hair, eh?"

"Uh. Yes. Anyway, as a longtime fan"—and disgruntled one-night stand—"I don't know how objective I can be. I was hoping you could grade his work for me."

Sanji drummed his fingers against his thigh for a moment. "Not a problem. You sure you don't want to just move him into one of my labs? I've got dozens of people who'd be willing to trade out."

"No." Jack grimaced. That was far too quick and far too adamant. "I mean, it's not necessary. No need to upset the current balance when this is just a minor thing."

"Right, right." At least Sanji had the decency to pretend he believed Jack. Not well, but he gave it a shot.

"Thank you."

Jack had to admit to a tiny niggle of worry Devlin was in over his head. Jack didn't want to destroy his plan for a second career, but shit. What if Devlin did poorly in archaeology? What if he flunked his other classes? What if music was all Devlin could reasonably do?

Get a grip, Johnson. Devlin was messing with his head, and this was precisely the reason he shouldn't be responsible for Devlin's grades.

"That everything?"

"Yes. Thank you."

Sanji left, and Jack stayed seated, feeling shaky and wrung out. At least he didn't feel faint, so he was one up on last week.

"I LOVE Italian food. Don't you? This is okay, isn't it?"

Devlin smiled fondly at Ken, just a happy little puppy wagging his tail. "Yes, this is great. I'm good with Italian." He'd said it a couple of times already, but Ken was so absurdly happy he couldn't bring himself to respond harshly.

"Good, good."

They hadn't left immediately after their lab—that would have been far too early for dinner—but instead planned to meet up at the library. Ken lived in one of the dorms, and he dropped off his school stuff. Devlin didn't have time to drop his bag off at home—if he got all the way home, there was no way he'd be leaving again to talk to Ken about this nebulous social club.

Instead he'd called the car service that the band used when they were doing shows and arranged for a driver to pick up his bag and drop it off at his place. Perhaps a little wasteful, but he really didn't want to be lugging crap around to a restaurant and maybe some sort of club or bar after.

Ken smiled nervously at him as they waited to be seated, and Devlin looked around. His first time at university had only lasted a year, but there was no way he'd ever have eaten at a place like this. Not that his family had been destitute or anything. Having him while they'd still been teenagers had made everything difficult. By the time Devlin started university at eighteen, they had good, stable jobs that they enjoyed, although they weren't ever going to get rich at them. But university students were supposed to live off boxed pasta, cheap ramen, and pizza. Devlin wouldn't have asked his parents for money to splurge on a restaurant, even one as modest as this one. He'd had a part-time job, but all that money had gone to musical equipment as he and Trent had been desperate to get recognition for Negative Impression.

He hoped Ken wasn't using similarly hoarded cash to pay for this meal. That was unacceptable. Devlin would pick up the tab and let Ken keep his money for something else. Even if Mom and Dad were paying expenses. And how many potential members got a dinner preview? Now that he thought about it in terms of resources, it did seem a little weird.

Maybe the social group itself had some sort of discretionary funds. In short order he'd know more, and he could worry about Ken's foolish spending later.

He was also going to have to dust off his rusty small-talk skills, because there was no way explaining any sort of social club would take up the entirety of dinner.

The hostess waved them forward, and Devlin gestured for Ken to precede him.

As they neared their table, Devlin tensed. The universe was definitely meddling in his business tonight, because their destination was the table beside Dr. Jack and another man. The only question was whether the fates were working for or against him.

"Time to roll the dice," Devlin whispered as the hostess stopped by their table with a smile on her face.

Ken recognized Dr. Jack before their professor noticed them and let out a bleat of distress and dithered about which seat to take. For someone Ken's age, it had to be nerve-wracking to consider having a meal next to an authority figure, one who had thus far shown himself to be a bit of a tyrant. Fighting to keep a grin off his face, Devlin gently pushed past Ken and sat down so he could spend the meal watching Dr. Jack. He only glanced at the other man, who wasn't necessarily a boyfriend. His identity didn't matter, although he could admit his presence caused an unpleasant wrench in Devlin's chest.

Devlin slouched in a relaxed manner before he spoke. "Well, hello there, Dr. Jack."

Jack nearly leaped right out of his chair, and Devlin conceded he might enjoy tonight.

"What… what… are you doing here?" Jack sputtered, and his companion craned his neck to get a good look at Devlin.

"Having dinner. Same as you." Ken was quietly having a meltdown across the way, but Devlin ignored him for the time being.

Jack took a couple of deep breaths. "You startled me."

"No shit." Devlin grinned, although the man next to him flinched. From the profanity? Devlin shook his head. Too delicate for Dr. Jack. He couldn't be the boyfriend, could he? He tilted his head in the blond's direction. "This the boyfriend?" He couldn't not ask. He'd been biting holes in his tongue trying to avoid asking personal questions at office hours, but the answer had weighed on his mind.

"This is my date, Matt. Second date."

Good. Nobody was too invested. "Ooh. Second date. Nice to meet you, second-date Matt. I'm Devlin." He reached an arm over to Matt's space, forcing him to cross a hand over his body to shake.

"Devlin." Matt's voice could have frozen lava. Devlin turned his attention back to Jack, smiling in the face of Jack's dark scowl.

"Matt, this is Devlin. And, uh…." Jack finally noticed Devlin was sitting with someone. Devlin wasn't a cradle robber, but in this instance he was so fucking happy that Ken could have been cast as an ethereal elf. He was tall, slim, and fair of face.

"Ken. You remember Ken, right?" Devlin prompted.

The scowl morphed into a glare, but slashes of red in Jack's cheeks attested to his emotional turmoil. Perhaps only because of encountering students during his private time, but Devlin hoped Jack didn't like seeing him out with a man, any more than Devlin liked seeing Jack with Matt.

"Yes, Ken. Of course. Ken, Matt, Matt, Ken. These are students of mine."

Out of the corner of his eye, Devlin saw Matt stare hard at the side of his face, but he ignored him. He didn't have to justify his age to any-fucking-one, least of all clean-cut boring Matt.

The arrival of a waiter drew his attention away, and they both ordered, although Ken did get carded before he could get a beer. Devlin bit back a sigh. Carded. Then again, Ken might only be nineteen. When Devlin had first started university he'd been eighteen, a year younger than Ontario's drinking age. If Ken was still in first year, and not just picking up a first-year course, he could very well be nineteen.

What the fuck was he doing?

"Isn't Ken a little young for you?" Jack sniped.

Oh yes. That's what he was doing, at least right this moment. Trying to annoy Jack as purposefully as if he'd leaned over and flicked him on the forehead.

How exactly was it the man didn't even have a five-o'clock shadow? Unusual for a man with black hair. Maybe Jack didn't have a lot of body hair…. But dinner was the wrong time for that sort of useless speculation.

"We're not on a date, sir," Ken stammered out, completely ruining the building jealousy. Dammit. Ken failed as a wingman.

"Oh. You're not?" Jack's expression smoothed out some.

"No. My social club, Excalibur, is holding a membership drive. I thought Devlin might be interested in it, so I was going to give him some information over dinner. The group meets later tonight, at seven."

This time, it was Devlin's cheeks that heated up. Epic fail for Ken as a wingman. Epic. Now Jack, out on his second date, knew Devlin didn't have anything better to do on a Friday night than audit social clubs, trolling for friends… or sex partners, depending on exactly what Excalibur meant to Ken and his buddies.

Did Ken even know Devlin was gay?

Jack didn't laugh, or even smirk. In fact, he looked distinctly unamused. "You don't say. A membership drive. Where you take a hot man out for dinner on a Friday night, with alcohol, under spurious pretext. Ken, surely you can do better than that."

"It's not spurious," Ken squeaked, but the way he wouldn't quite meet Devlin's eyes confirmed Jack's take on events.

"Slick, kid, very slick." Devlin stared at Ken. He'd more or less tricked Devlin into going on a date, and Devlin kind of admired him for it. Ken, for all his fine-featured beauty, clearly didn't have a lot of self-confidence. Unfortunately, Devlin didn't admire him enough to actually date him, though. "But I'm afraid Dr. Jack here is right. You're cute, kid, but way too young for me. I'm sorry."

Ken shifted in his chair, like he was ready to bolt, and Devlin realized he'd done a shitty thing in front of an audience.

"Hey, hey." He used his most calming tones, trying to channel his mother, who could always calm him down. He reached across and grabbed Ken's hand and squeezed. "Don't go anywhere. We've ordered. Let's have a nice meal, as friends, okay? And this group… it is real, right?"

Ken nodded frantically.

"Okay then. Is it something you think I'd like? Is it something you wouldn't mind me being there, even if we're only friends and not dating?"

"Maybe." Ken shrugged. "I like it. I'd be happy if you wanted to join."

"Right, then. So we eat, you tell me about the club, and we'll see if it's something I want to test out."

That got him a tiny grateful smile, although Ken did drain half his beer as soon as it arrived on the table. Devlin glanced up to see Jack with a soft, bemused expression on his face. He'd never once seen Jack like that, and it made him wonder if he'd look like that after sex, all blissed out. Devlin shifted in his chair, hoping no one realized he was chubbing up at the table for another man's date. While he was apparently on his own ambush date.

Matt cleared his throat. "Well, as entertaining as this has been, we'd better get going, Jack, if we're going to make the movie."

Dick.

"What movie are you seeing?" Devlin just couldn't help himself.

"Something with subtitles. Italian." Jack waved his hand over the table to indicate it had been a bit of a theme. "Matt thinks I'll like it."

With some effort, Devlin held back a derisive snort. Maybe it had been listening to hours of Jack lecturing, but something in his inflection told Devlin Matt was terribly wrong about Jack's taste in movies. It definitely wasn't subtitled art house films and Devlin wanted to know.

Jack finished the last of his red wine, which Devlin assumed was a chianti ordered by Matt, and stood to go, a hint of heightened color still in his throat.

"Devlin, Ken. I'll see you next week."

Too bad. Devlin could have taunted Jack all night, but that wasn't fair to Ken. Or Matt, although Devlin didn't much care what Matt thought about it all.

Their appetizers arrived, and Devlin put some bruschetta onto his plate. "Okay, Ken. Hit me. What's this club all about?"

JACK'S HANDS twitched over the stack of exercise sheets that Sanji had handed in that morning. It shouldn't matter how well Devlin had done, and yet the curiosity was killing him. He rarely had any emotional investment in a student's academic progress, but he wanted Devlin to succeed. Mostly. There was still a tiny, dark core of him that thought it might be okay if Devlin failed spectacularly. If he learned that things didn't just miraculously get served up on a silver platter.

He sort of hated that part of himself, and every time Devlin did something nice, it chipped away at that dark part. But it wasn't gone entirely, and he didn't know if it ever would go away, regardless of how guilty it made him feel.

The papers shuffled almost on their own, and not like he was restlessly sorting through them. His life had become complicated in some rather unexpected ways. Today, he'd been looking forward to Devlin's intense, heated looks during the lecture. Seeing Devlin be a really good guy on Friday—and make it clear he wasn't dating that twink—had made the Italian movie almost bearable. On the other hand, seeing Devlin during his date had split his focus, and again he hadn't given Matt a fair shake. If he didn't keep having weird encounters with Devlin, Matt might have the makings of a great boyfriend.

Matt might not understand Crimson Corrosion, though. Saturday had been their first gig since Devlin Waters had shown up in Jack's class, and Jack readily admitted it had been weird. He channeled all the good things he remembered from past concerts, and for the first time in years, he let himself think about Devlin—Blade—while he sang. Everyone agreed—it had been one of the most vibrant shows they'd done in a long time.

Given his track record so far, Jack half expected Devlin to show up at the gig, and had ended up being both relieved and disappointed. He really didn't know how Devlin would feel about Crimson Corrosion when he was calling himself unemployed. Hell, he might have hated the idea of a tribute band regardless of his status with Negative Impression.

Jack sighed and glanced at the clock. Only a few more minutes until Devlin showed up. He frowned. Now he was expecting Devlin, relying on him, to show up like clockwork. It had only been a couple of weeks, for fuck's sake.

His gaze dropped the papers, and he groaned. Devlin's exercise was right on top. Yup, his life had gotten strangely complicated. He flipped up the cover page to find the grade at the end of the second page. A+. He smiled. A simple grade shouldn't make him so pleased, but it did, probably because he was an idiot. Nevertheless, he skimmed through Devlin's answers, but Sanji hadn't cut Devlin any breaks because Jack had been a stupid fanboy.

"Hey there."

Jack fumbled with the exercise before bundling the whole stack and shoving them in his desk drawer. Friday would be soon enough for Devlin to see his grade, and he didn't exactly want to explain what he was doing.

"Hi."

Devlin dropped into the chair, his leg draped over the arm. There were times Jack decided he did that to try and entice Jack with his substantial package, but by now, he sort of realized Devlin sprawled like a lazy lion just because that was Devlin.

For a heart-stopping second, he wondered if Devlin sprawled the same way in bed, if he stole more than his fair share, or if he was a cuddler. He hadn't had a chance to find out, and never would know. Thinking about it wasn't going to get him past his issues with Devlin.

"How was your date on Friday?"

Jack shrugged. There wasn't really enough room in his head for Matt when Devlin sat right in front of him. "It was a date. More importantly, how was yours?"

As much as he'd hated the idea of Devlin dating anyone—and he hadn't really considered that Devlin might date whereas Blade only fucked—it had been quite entertaining when Devlin realized that yes, he was on a date.

"I said on Friday. That kid is too young for me."

He'd said it, and Jack wanted to believe it. "That was a nice thing you did." Not at first. His first words had been abrupt, blunt. But he'd quickly made up for it, yet more proof he was a man who made mistakes but—probably—wasn't a bad person.

Devlin shrugged. "My mom would have fucking killed me."

"Your mom?" Of course Blade hadn't popped out on a stage somewhere, fully formed, guitar in hand, but somehow in all his fanboying, he'd never actually considered his parents. What he was like as a small boy. What sort of environment he'd grown up in. Every day made Devlin the man more real and more relatable than Blade the bassist of Negative Impression.

Devlin looked slightly abashed. "My mom's a good person, and she'd be pissed if I'd hurt that poor kid because of careless words." Some other expression crossed over his face, one that Jack couldn't read, but it looked a lot like self-loathing. He wanted to ask, but they really didn't know each other well enough for that.

"What about your dad?"

A muscle ticked in Devlin's jaw. "He died a few years back. Cancer."

"I'm so sorry." Guilt attacked like tiger claws. No wonder Jack had hurt him so badly that first time he'd shown up in Jack's office. He was coming back to university to please his dead father. Jack knew a little bit about trying to please a father, but he had a feeling Devlin's dad wasn't anything like his own.

"Thanks. What about you? Your parents still around?"

Fucking hell. He hadn't really expected turnabout in this conversation. Usually when his students told him about their personal lives, they were too intimidated to ask about his. Devlin didn't know the meaning of the word intimidation. At least, not by the likes of one ordinary archaeology professor.

"My dad's in assisted living for Alzheimer's. My mom took off when I was eight, haven't seen her since."

"That's awful. I'm so sorry." Devlin frowned in sympathy.

Surreal. Very fucking surreal. Also depressing. He couldn't forget depressing, and he wasn't ready to bare his innermost feelings to this man.

"Um. So what was Ken's social club all about?"

Devlin blinked at him for a minute, as though processing the abrupt change of subject. "Funny thing. It actually was right up my alley. Excalibur plays collectible card and deck-building games."

Jack frowned. "Cards? Like poker? Gambling?" He didn't know what the university policy was on gambling. There might be some sort of fuzzy regulations that allowed for fund-raisers and raffles and whatnot, but he had a feeling poker might be well beyond regulations.

Devlin laughed. "No. Well, I don't think it would be classed that way. They host tournaments, and I guess proceeds go to various charities. Heard of Magic: The Gathering?"

"Yeah, sure."

"Well, that's one of the games they play. And I've been playing it longer than Ken has been alive." Devlin exaggerated his grimace, surprising a laugh out of Jack.

"Ouch. That had to hurt. Let me guess… he started out by explaining things in some roundabout way like you were an idiot."

Devlin tapped his nose. "Exactly. I did feel just a bit like the old man on the mountain. But it was fun, and the tournaments are apparently open to the public, not restricted to students like the regular meets are. I might not be the oldest dude at a tournament."

"So, you're good at it?" Not in a million years would he have guessed Devlin played Magic: The Gathering. Now he also wanted to know if the rest of the band played it too, or if Devlin had other, nonband friends he broke out the cards with.

"Eh. I actually haven't kept up with it for a long time. The problem with collectibles is that they keep coming out with new things to collect. Got to be a bit onerous after a while. But it doesn't matter if I'm good or not. Pay my registration fee, contribute a little to a charity, have some fun. Doesn't matter if I win."

Why, oh why did he keep finding these things out about Devlin? Each day he felt more like an asshole for hanging on to this resentment, and yet he hadn't quite found the strength to forgive Devlin. Nor could he forget how attractive he found Devlin. Every interaction only made him more aware of Devlin's scent, his voice, the heat of his body. At night he'd remember the good parts of having sex with Blade as he came all over his fist.

This was the complete opposite of what he wanted to happen. Devlin was a pipe dream; Matt was a reasonable boyfriend choice. He'd already agreed to another date on Saturday night. Devlin was off-limits, and he was going to have to stay that way for the sake of Jack's sanity.

He swept a glance along Devlin's body. Yes. Off-limits. But he was already doubting his sanity, spending so much time with such a temptation.

They chatted for a few minutes more, but another student showed up, cutting their time short. Jack was a little resentful. He'd come to enjoy Devlin's office-hour visitations, but the more time went by, the more likely they'd be interrupted as more students realized they needed help. One of his third-year classes was heading into their first exam; exams and papers always triggered a panicked surge in student visits in the days leading up to them.

As always, Devlin stood up and left, and Jack remained, staring regretfully at Devlin's ass.

CHAPTER SEVEN

JACK STOOD by the dance floor, sipping at his ginger ale. He'd driven to meet Matt for their date, since it was Saturday, and not just an extension of his workday, where he used public transit. The one glass of wine he'd had with dinner—another of Matt's choices—was his limit, but somehow, he'd agreed to come back here, to Ciao, for more dancing. The music wasn't any better than the last time Matt had dragged him here, but Matt was definitely enjoying himself out on the dance floor.

He had to get out of this gracefully. He was fooling himself that he and Matt would work out, and he'd gotten the feeling over dinner that Matt subscribed to the "third date equals sex" rule. He hadn't met anyone, gay or straight, who held hard and fast to that as a guideline for when sex should happen, but Matt had made some heavy-handed innuendo over dinner, and Jack just wasn't feeling it.

Then again, it wouldn't be the first time he'd given someone a hand job or let them blow him just to avoid an awkward rejection, but he sort of thought Matt was expecting an invitation home, and that definitely wasn't happening. In the meantime, he was stuck in this club with music that made him dead inside.

Jack scanned the tables lining the club's walls. Even those people not dancing were having more fun than he was. Groups of people sat around chatting—not sure how they managed it in this din—or kissed or…. Jack squinted. The strobing purple and green lights didn't do anything to aid his vision. He casually started moving closer to the table that held one man, resting his head on a hand and looking as dejected as Jack had seen anyone.

Closer, closer. Surely that wasn't Devlin. Again. Showing up at yet another of Jack's dates. This had to be a sign, didn't it?

He plunked down in the seat next to Devlin.

"So, are you following me?" He made sure to sound teasing, or at least as teasing as it was possible to be when yelling above whatever pop princess currently entertained the dancing masses.

Devlin turned a bleary look on him, and seconds later, the lights settled, leaving Devlin in dim light but mostly visible.

Jack sucked in a gasp. Pain was evident on every inch of Devlin's face, and he was drowning his sorrows in booze, judging by the empty glasses around him and, well, the smell.

"Devlin. What's wrong? Are you okay?"

"Oh. Hi, Jack."

Well this wasn't good. "Hi, Devlin. What happened? Why are you here?"

Devlin shrugged, and his head almost slid off his hand. "Some of the kids from Excalibur invited me out."

Excalibur? Oh right. Ken's gaming group. Devlin had mentioned at Wednesday's office hours he was probably going to attend both nights this week, unless something else turned up.

"That's nice." Where the fuck were they? "This doesn't seem like your kind of place."

Devlin let out an exaggerated sigh. "It's not. Not at all."

"Yeah, not my kind of place either." Not that Devlin knew that about him.

"I didn't want to be alone tonight." Devlin's voice was small and sad, and Jack couldn't help but notice that he was alone. Maybe his new friends were on the dance floor, but didn't one of them notice that Devlin was broken? Considering his usual swagger and overabundance of confidence, this version of Devlin, practically curled into a protective position, should have raised a cohort of red flags.

He could not in good conscience leave Devlin here like this, and it had nothing to do with weaseling out of his date early. That was more like his reward for taking care of someone who clearly needed help.

"There you are." Matt materialized beside him and sat down. "I thought you were going to come and dance."

Uh, not in this space-time continuum. "Sorry. I saw a friend. I think I need to get him home. Something's happened."

Matt frowned at Devlin. "This guy again? I thought you said he was a student. And he's drunk. That's what's happened. He's more than old enough to take care of himself."

Jack gritted his teeth. "I'm sorry, Matt. I can't leave him here like this. I need to take him home."

"You're taking him home." This wasn't going well at all.

"Look, I'll call you later."

Matt's lip curled up in a sneer. "Don't bother." He pushed away from the table and barreled back onto the dance floor.

"Asshole," Devlin muttered. Jack smothered a laugh; he wasn't even sure Devlin was sober enough to recall meeting Matt. But yeah, he kind of was an asshole, no matter how much rosewater Jack had tossed on him.

"C'mon. There's a coffee shop near here, open late. Let's see if we can sober you up some."

"M'kay."

Surprisingly pliable, Devlin let Jack help him to his feet. He was wearing another skintight T-shirt, and nothing else around the table looked like it belonged to him. "Did you bring a jacket?"

"Jacket?"

"Yes. It's October now. Sometimes it gets cold at night."

Devlin rolled his eyes and sent his head flopping, nearly falling to the ground. "No need for sarcasm."

That sounded more sober than Devlin looked.

"Then answer the question."

"What question?"

Christ on a cracker. "Did you bring a jacket?"

"No."

Wrangling drunks was never easy, but Devlin did follow Jack with a minimum of fuss. He didn't much want to try and figure out where Devlin lived until he was a little more sober, or he might end up driving halfway across Scarberia on bad directions.

IN THE Second Cup, Devlin squinted at the relatively bright lights and frowned.

"Too bright," he mumbled. He'd been fighting the burn in his eyes all night, and this only made it harder. No matter how much alcohol he ingested, though, he couldn't forget. Couldn't make anything better. The pain battled the alcoholic haze, and the hurt was winning.

Jack let out an exasperated sigh. "We can go sit in my car. I'm parked close, and at least there's a heater in the car."

Was it cold out? He couldn't remember, but Jack's arm was warm against him.

Devlin wobbled a bit as they stood in line, and leaned against Jack, who was a lot stronger than Devlin expected. He turned a nose into Jack's neck.

"You smell great." Not the same scent he had at work, and watery annoyance swam in his mind at the thought that Jack had worn different, delicious cologne for *Matt*. Once the great sea of booze had drained some, he'd probably be quite pissed off. Then again, Matt had buggered off somewhere, and Jack was here with him.

"What do you want?"

At this second? He wanted to bite Jack's neck, then suck up a mark on all that pale skin.

"Devlin? How do you take your coffee?"

"Dunno."

Jack's neck vibrated against Devlin's nose. Even his exasperation felt good.

"Fine. A large double double, and a large black, double sugar."

Smelled good and smart, Jack was. Putting a double or even a single helping of cream in his coffee wouldn't mix well at all with the bourbon. He thought. Normally Devlin got a frouffy drink, but he couldn't remember what it was called. Had whipped cream, but that was also a bad idea. Probably.

When the coffees arrived, Jack stared at the two cups and then glanced at Devlin. "Can I have a tray? I'm not sure I have enough hands."

The barista giggled, but Devlin didn't know why Jack needed another hand.

On the way back to the car, Devlin realized Jack needed a third hand—uh… his second hand?—to keep him from tripping over cracks in the sidewalk, stray garbage, and his own feet.

Jack helped him into the passenger seat, then rounded the car to get in the driver's side. Shivers skated up and down his spine. Didn't he have a jacket? Once Jack got the coffees seated in the cup holders, turned on the car, and set the heater on full, Devlin squirmed as far over the center console as he could and leaned against Jack's shoulder. Warm and smelled fucking awesome.

Devlin flung an arm across Jack, hand landing perilously close to his dick, making Jack chuckle nervously.

Jack wrapped his arm around Devlin, lightly stroking the chilled flesh of his bare arm. Soothing. If only Jack could make him forget.

"You should drink this coffee while it's hot."

"In a minute." If Jack had an old car with bench seats, Devlin would probably be fully wrapped around him, despite the underlying thought that he shouldn't be doing this. Shouldn't be touching Jack like this. Shouldn't want to strip him naked and fuck him senseless.

"Okay, in a minute. Want to tell me what's wrong?" Jack's voice was gentle, coaxing, like Devlin was a skittish horse.

Devlin didn't talk about it. Devlin never wanted to talk about it ever again, but there was something about Jack. Kind, warm, sometimes prickly Jack, who'd never known Trent. He'd kept everything locked up for months, but tonight was like a witching moon. The memory of Trent was too strong this night, and alcohol had dissolved the locks.

Devlin heaved out a breath. "I couldn't face today alone. But I couldn't call anyone who knew him."

"Him who?"

"I… was in a band. No one you would have heard of. Me and my best friend, Trent, started it." Even that simple memory was like sandpaper on a sunburn. His nose tingled, and he swallowed heavily. He thought he'd shed all the tears in him at the funeral, but he hadn't realized it was the other milestones, the milestones he'd have to endure alone… those were the ones that scraped at the soul.

Jack murmured soothingly, letting Devlin ramble. For all that Jack would look perfect dressed in black and dancing to Devlin's music, he was equally sure Jack didn't have a nodding acquaintance with the combination industrial and punk music Negative Impression had found success with.

"We met in kindergarten. Both only children, we became brothers, or near as. Formed the band in high school. Just the two of us at first, but eventually we found Luke and Mo. Did a few gigs, got some recognition, started touring in Europe." The sandpaper became glass shards, tearing at wounds imperfectly healed.

"Ended up doing the music thing for more than twenty years. And it was good."

Fuck, fuck, fuck. Devlin clenched his fists, fingernails digging into his palms. He didn't want to say it aloud, but he didn't think he could stop. Getting drunk tonight hadn't been smart. Unless he'd managed to drink to oblivion, and he sure as shit wasn't *there*.

"Then one day, we were in Germany, and he missed rehearsal. Didn't answer his phone. Had the hotel manager open his room, but it was too late. I know everyone thought it was drugs at first. Even I was afraid of it, although I'd never known Trent to do drugs."

Devlin sniffed and buried his face against Jack's shoulder, tears streaming uncontrollably down his face and soaking Jack's shirt. Jack shuddered briefly but didn't let go.

Devlin could remember when the officials came and spoke to them. The German police—he couldn't remember what they were called, but they spoke English in clipped, impersonal tones. The suggestion that Trent had overdosed, and that somehow made his loss… less tragic. Devlin had just about lost his shit to the point of almost getting arrested. Deep in his heart, he knew Trent hadn't been using, because he'd never used—none of the band did. But he didn't care, and he wanted answers. Demanded answers. Made a nuisance of himself when he wasn't raging in a cold, beige hotel room. Drugs or not, after that night, Devlin might never be whole again.

"I'm so sorry, God, I'm so fucking sorry," Jack whispered, his voice breaking just a bit, letting Devlin know he wasn't alone. Not tonight.

Devlin dragged in a shaky, soggy breath, his throat tight from tears both shed and unshed. "Turned out it was an aneurysm. Quick. Didn't have a chance, really. We didn't have any chance to prepare. To… even consider it could happen."

Jack hugged him closer, and Devlin's chest heaved a bit. One more bit to get out, and for whatever reason, Devlin couldn't fight the compulsion to speak.

"Friends—brothers—for all those years, and today is his birthday. The first one I haven't spent with him in thirty-five years." No longer able fight it, angry, wracking sobs grasped him, and he shook in Jack's arms.

Even when it seemed like Devlin might do this until all the moisture in his body exited in tears, leaving him a desiccated husk of a man, Jack only held him tighter and rocked him gently.

Eventually, though, Devlin's tears dried up, but he had no idea how long he'd cried all over Jack. He was warm all through for the first time tonight. He hiccupped a couple of times and sat up. Jack reached into the glove box. A few seconds rummaging returned a handful of fast-food napkins. Jack kept one but handed the rest of them to Devlin.

Before Devlin could make use of them, Jack wiped Devlin's cheeks down. Devlin used the other napkins to blow his nose, all the skin in his face swollen, hot, and sensitive. Breathing would be tricky for a bit, as he was every bit as congested as if he had a bad head cold.

Cleanup taken care of, Jack reached for the coffee. "Want some of this? It's still a little warm. I wish I had some water for you, but this is wet at least." And caffeinated, which Devlin could use about now.

"Thanks." With a thickened, scratchy voice, the word was barely understandable. He sipped gingerly at the brew without wincing. At least with good coffee it was still palatable when it wasn't hot. Jack swallowed a few mouthfuls of his own.

"Why didn't you call Luke or Mo?"

Exhaustion kept him from bursting into tears again, but it hurt enough that he wanted to. Devlin had broken bones and dislocated his shoulder and had his appendix out. And he'd go through all that and more, because physical pain was nothing compared to this. "I just can't face them. It's too hard. We've been family for twenty years, and every time I'm with them, I'm reminded I'll never see Trent again. I haven't met up with either of them."

Jack's eyes started blinking rapidly, and he bit his lip. After a moment, Jack took a deep breath and spoke again. "Since the funeral? Surely they've called or something. They're both from around here, right?"

Devlin glanced down at the cup in his hands and started picking at the cardboard sleeve. "They call sometimes. Email. But I let it go to voicemail. Ignore them."

"You know, they're probably hurting too."

"Yeah. I guess." But the weight of their grief, the slap of pity in their eyes would be more than he could take. Devlin drank a bit more coffee, then slumped back against Jack again. The alcohol was definitely wearing off. "You know, we all used fake names in the band. Trent and I both had names that more suited a hero in a romance novel than a badass punk rocker. Trent Halloran and Devlin Waters. Sounded like the Regency romances my mom reads. Both of us just used the nicknames we already had, Blade and Reaver. When Luke and Mo joined, they liked the idea and became Dragon and Snake. Hardly any of our fans even knew our real names, and we were just as happy like that."

Devlin fell silent again. Talking about Trent hurt, but they'd built up a lifetime of good memories, and he needed someone else to know that. He stirred and drank some more coffee, which was now cold, but as Jack had said, it was wet, and he needed something for his parched throat. Jack had already given up on his coffee.

There was a time when Devlin carried water and throat lozenges with him wherever he went, but saving his voice was no longer necessary. He was never going to sing again. The part of him that took joy in music had died with Trent.

"How'd you come up with those nicknames?"

Devlin laughed, but it was a stuffy, sad sound, not his true laugh.

"When we were… eight or nine, I forget, I wanted to be a circus performer. Specifically a knife thrower."

Jack's eyes widened. "Oh shit."

"Yeah, exactly. I still have a scar on my foot from where I accidentally lodged one of Trent's mother's steak knives. I thought she and my mom were going to lose their fucking minds. Once the ER doc had assured everyone I wasn't going to bleed to death and I was all patched up, well, the stitches and all seemed kinda cool to both me and Trent, and he started calling me Blade."

The chaos had been incredible. Mrs. Halloran abject in apologizing, but neither of Devlin's parents had blamed her for Devlin's stupidity. And that his actions had been stupid had been pounded into his head via extensive lectures as soon as his stitches had come out.

"What about Trent?"

Devlin sniffed again and used one of the crumpled, damp napkins and blew his nose again. "Trent loved cookies. He could find them where the fuck ever his parents had them stashed. And his parents were British. Called him their sneaky biscuit reaver, which eventually got shortened to Reaver. And voilà, badass punk rocker names."

Most times Trent stole them for Devlin. When they'd first become friends, his parents had been struggling financially, to the point that cookies were an occasional luxury, not a standard pantry staple like they were in Trent's house. Mrs. Halloran was a responsible parent, and although she was happy to give Devlin a cookie or two when he showed up at their house, she wasn't about to let him or her son gorge on them. Trent had a different opinion on the matter and thought it was a tragedy that Devlin didn't have cookies at home and hadn't even tasted some of Trent's favorites.

He leaned his face against the cold glass of the passenger-side window, the chill easing some of the ferocious heat in his face. He wanted this night over.

TRENT'S BIRTHDAY. Jack might have been a fanboy, but that particular scrap of information had long since left his memory, if he'd even known it. He'd thought Devlin had seemed… off in the lab yesterday but hadn't given it another thought, and he hated himself for that.

Devlin had been silent long enough that Jack assumed there would be no more revelations. Honestly, though, Jack didn't know if his heart could stand anything else. He'd thought his one-night stand with a drunken Devlin had been heart-wrenching, but he simply hadn't known the meaning of the term back then. Devlin and alcohol made a dangerous combination, in completely unexpected ways.

The heater didn't make up for having Devlin curled around him as much as humanly possible with the center console in the way, and Jack found himself slightly chilled. Having Devlin all touchy-feely, nuzzling him, and even comforting him had felt so fucking good that it bordered on tortuous. Under the bourbon haze, Devlin had also smelled good, and before the tears had started, Jack had been sorely tempted to revisit that night four years ago. But last time, they had both been drunk; with only Devlin drunk and their new status as professor and student, it would have been an unforgivable lapse, taking advantage in the worst way.

But then Devlin told him about Trent. Jack hadn't known they'd been friends so long. Hadn't considered—but should have—how devastating the loss of Trent had to have been, for the whole band and Devlin in particular. He was an utter fucking dick, once again failing to recognize Devlin as a human being. As he'd held Devlin, he'd cried too, unable to help himself. His eyes still burned, but they couldn't be as bloodshot as Devlin's.

The aneurysm hadn't been publicized anywhere that Jack knew of. He had to admit, he'd assumed an overdose as well, and he was ashamed for it.

"C'mon, buckle up. Let's get you home to sleep this off."

"You don't have to drive me home."

"Devlin, seriously, I couldn't live with myself if I didn't see you safely home."

Fucking hell. Jack hadn't even considered, not once, that it had been less than a year since Trent died. That Devlin had been knocking around, looking for direction, seeking new friends, and still grieving.

If Jack hadn't found him at Ciao, he didn't want to think about how this night might have gone for Devlin. Alcohol and grief could be a lethal combination.

Even worse, the only people in the world, aside from Trent's family—assuming he had any left—who could understand Devlin's grief were the other band members, and Devlin wouldn't let himself find comfort with them. Jesus Christ. Jack's eyes burned again, and he surreptitiously swiped at them with his sleeve.

He was so fucking glad he'd found Devlin tonight. Devlin had been in desperate need of a friend, and Jack was happy to fill that role.

"It's far." The silence had gone on so long that Jack had thought for a moment Devlin had fallen asleep. Or passed out.

"Just give me the address for the GPS."

Jack punched it in. It was far, but it was fairly close to Stephanie's place. If he didn't feel like driving back home after dropping Devlin off, he'd call her and crash there. If she hadn't gone out, she'd be pissed at getting woken up, but she'd forgive him. Eventually. If he told her the story of how Trent and Devlin got their nicknames, she'd forgive him immediately.

Jack had thought he was going to fucking die from the cute. In a million years, with a billion guesses, Jack would never have figured out how Trent and Devlin had come up with their "badass" pseudonyms. Not that he'd tell Stephanie without Devlin's permission, though. That personal detail definitely wasn't for indiscriminate sharing.

In between short anecdotes about Trent and life on the road as a touring band, Devlin dozed. The inside look had Jack riveted, and he wondered, briefly, if he should have told Devlin he knew who he was and knew who the band was. But he wasn't sure Devlin was in any shape to retain information, and there never seemed to be a good time to wedge in those details.

The traffic heading out of downtown and into Oakville wasn't too heavy, and it only took about forty-five minutes. Devlin was asleep when Jack turned into his drive.

This couldn't be the right place, could it? There was a gate. And the house was enormous. Jack knew Negative Impression had been successful but not to this degree. Or rather, he never knew exactly how success translated to actual income.

He reached over and shook Devlin's shoulder. "Wake up. We're here." Maybe. Perhaps he should have been worried about driving blindly all over Oakville instead. Either way, he needed Devlin awake to either give him the correct address or to give him the gate code.

"Hmm, what?"

"I need a gate code." Acid test, if this wasn't Devlin's house.

"It's 5912."

Jack opened the window and shivered as a gust of cold wind swept into the car. October it might be, but it was still a little early for such frigid temperatures.

Somewhat to his surprise, the gate swung open, and Jack drove in. It was too dark to see the water, but he'd turned off Lakeshore in the direction of the lake. If he wasn't completely turned around, this was beachfront property. Not only was the house enormous but the property was worth a fucking pretty penny.

"Just park in front of the garage."

Jack followed instructions, then got out of the car to help Devlin to the front door. Devlin clutched him close, face pressed against his neck.

"Please don't go. I don't want to be alone."

Jack glanced up at the house. A person could get lost in a house like this, and he didn't really want to leave Devlin alone, especially not after that throaty plea. He suspected that things could easily get heated between them, if he let it, but he was determined to get Devlin to sleep, and that was all.

"I'll stay."

Devlin squeezed him tight, then handed him his keys. Inside the door, Jack kicked off his shoes, not wanting to scuff anything expensive.

As they made their clumsy way to Devlin's bedroom, Jack shook his head. Ten years ago, he would have given his left nut to get unfettered access to Blade's home. He was still interested—far more so than he'd been a month ago—but his primary concern was getting Devlin safely into bed to sleep off an emotionally exhausting day.

The place echoed like a mausoleum, and Jack didn't blame Devlin one bit for not wanting to be alone here. In the best of moods, Jack might have second thoughts about it.

In Devlin's bedroom, Jack flipped back the covers and let Devlin sit down on the mattress while he stripped off everything but his boxer briefs. This might be a mistake, but he wanted to be close to keep an eye on Devlin. For safety, and not for any prurient curiosity about how Devlin shared a bed.

Devlin didn't make any move to get undressed, so Jack pulled off his shoes and T-shirt, exposing those tattoos he'd found so sexy—and still did. He licked his lips, the memory still so fresh. He sighed. Trust Devlin to complicate Jack's third date with another man.

He contemplated Devlin's tight jeans as Devlin leered up at him and clutched at Jack's ass. His cock thickened, not realizing Devlin's mouth wasn't at crotch level for sexy fun times. Those jeans posed a serious problem. Devlin wouldn't—couldn't possibly—sleep comfortably with them on, but Jack knew from experience that Devlin could easily be going commando.

It was a risk he needed to take.

"C'mon. Lie back." Jack coaxed Devlin onto the bed, flat on his back.

"Mmm. You got a nickname, Dr. Jack?"

Jack lifted an eyebrow as he gingerly undid Devlin's button and slid down the zipper, trying desperately to ignore the solid heft of an erection pressing against the denim.

"Besides Dr. Jack?" Which he didn't like, but he liked it more than pussy or faggot, which his father had called him. Still did on occasion at the assisted living place, even on days when he couldn't remember who Jack was. Didn't count as a nickname. Jack had never been able to live up to his father's expectations, nor had he been able to escape the blame for his mother leaving, at least in his father's eyes.

"Dr. Jack. Dr. Jack Johnson." Devlin's voice petered out at the end of Jack's last name. A boring name, nothing like Devlin's romance hero name.

He tugged at the bottom of Devlin's jeans and averted his eyes from Devlin's groin, hoping to avoid any additional intimate knowledge of Devlin's cock.

"Jack Johnson. Jack Johnson." Apparently Devlin wasn't quite asleep. Jack kept tugging, the slide of denim slow but steady.

"JJ!" Devlin almost shouted, startling Jack into looking at him, past the prominent hard cock. He bit back a groan. Goddamn Devlin, making his heart hurt and making his cock hard all in one day, when Jack was still supposed to hate—dislike—the man.

"What now?"

Devlin grinned down at him and stroked his cock. Jack sucked in a breath. Devlin didn't wax anymore, and the trimmed bush was every bit as enticing as completely bare. "JJ. You can be JJ. Nicknames are good. Fun."

As much as Jack liked the way Devlin called him JJ, he was hugely thankful Devlin likely wouldn't remember most of this night.

"Stop that. You need sleep," Jack scolded, but it was more for his own benefit than Devlin's.

"Mmm. Sex first. Then sleep."

"No sex."

Devlin's wicked smile suggested he thought otherwise, but Jack couldn't cave. Devlin was beautiful, gorgeous, and Jack wouldn't be able to resent him if he hated himself for taking advantage of Devlin in this state.

Another tug set Devlin's legs free, and resolutely not looking—again—at Devlin's cock or tattoos, Jack glanced around the room. The door to the bathroom was exactly what he needed.

"Where are you going?"

Jack ignored the plaintive question each time it was repeated while he ran cold water and filled a cup. He flipped open the medicine cabinet but didn't see any acetaminophen for the headache Devlin would undoubtedly have in the morning. He returned to the bedroom and put the cup on the nightstand beside Devlin.

"You should probably drink this now."

"Okay, JJ." Devlin twisted around, cock leading the way, propped himself up on an elbow, and swiftly downed the water. Jack refilled it so Devlin would have it later, then got into bed on the other side.

Immediately Devlin plastered himself to his back, arms tight around him, lips at his neck, and cock prodding his ass.

Jack bit back another groan as his own cock hardened fully. If Jack lost his mind, it would be all Devlin's fault.

Devlin's lips moved lightly across his nape, the fine hairs there standing at attention. Then Devlin started stroking his chest and belly, slowly edging to Jack's waistband. "JJ," he whispered, making Jack shiver.

"Seriously, Devlin, we can't do this." If only he'd been able to imbue his voice with any sort of conviction.

Then Devlin huffed out a breath, warm and humid along his neck, and his arms slackened.

Jack held still for a moment. Devlin started snoring, soft breathy exhalations, and Jack sighed in relief. Not disappointment. Relief.

Not exactly how he'd expected his date night to go, but Jack didn't have a single regret about choosing Devlin over Matt.

Chapter Eight

JACK BLINKED awake, eyes grainy and sore. Was he getting sick? His throat felt fine. Then he squinted. The dresser—which was not his—sat way too fucking far from the bed.

Arms tightened about his waist, and Jack turned his face into the pillow—which smelled like Devlin, damn him—and muffled a groan.

So, so much new information last night. And he'd come close to breaking down and taking what Devlin had been offering. His morning wood perked up at the scent and feel of Devlin surrounding him, but the breathy snores told him Devlin still slept on. In addition to a metric fuck-ton of personal details of Devlin's life and friendship with Trent, he now knew how Devlin slept with someone else in the bed. Jack had been held tight all night, and it was too sweet for words. Jack had slept like he'd never slept before. This was the comfort he'd been seeking all his life, and he couldn't believe Devlin was the one who gave it to him.

Like four years ago, though, Jack was only going to get a single night's taste, because… where was he going to go from here? They weren't right for each other. Even if Jack had been wavering in his conviction that Devlin was an ass who played fast and loose with people's emotions, this house showed how different they were. Would Devlin be able to understand the lower middle-class household Jack had grown up in? The ridiculously modest-by-comparison apartment he lived in. The frugality by which Jack lived.

Sometime during the night, his subconscious had revealed the biggest stumbling block of all. It was possible—probable—that Devlin had been in love with Trent.

How could Jack even compete with that?

Desolation sent a chill through him, closely followed by a noisy grumble from a stomach too long denied. He craned his head up looking for the bedside clock. Noon! Shit. It was way later than he'd thought. He never slept more than eight hours, but apparently after Devlin dragged him through an emotional wringer, then held him tight, ten hours was achievable.

He tried to wiggle out of Devlin's grip. "Don't go," Devlin whispered, still mostly asleep.

Poor bastard was going to have one hell of a hangover. Drinking was bad enough without all the crying.

"I need to get something to eat."

"No food in the kitchen. Go to the guesthouse."

Guesthouse? "You have to let me go first."

"No."

Jack rolled his eyes. Surely Devlin wasn't still drunk. But it was clear his obstinacy was deeply ingrained and came as naturally as breathing.

"I'm starving. Let me go grab something."

"Bring some back?"

Oh for fuck's sake. If Devlin was going to keep up the sweetness, Jack needed to learn how to tell him no. "Fine. Let me up."

Devlin rolled over, and the snores started up again.

Jack pulled on the clothes he'd left strewn on the floor and considered the lithe form under the covers. The smartest thing to do would be to just leave. Go to work on Monday, pretend this never happened. There was a time when he imagined doing that very thing as a petty revenge.

But he couldn't do it. Just could not do it. He'd been holding a stupid grudge for too long, and Devlin could wake in a fragile state. Jack couldn't be responsible for adding another smidgeon of pain. Not when the alternative was so easy. And if that meant *Jack* would get hurt somewhere down the line, then that was a risk he had to take. It was too late; feelings had taken root. Real feelings, not the sham infatuation of a fanboy.

His stomach growled again.

Food first, before he worried about anything. Devlin had to be kidding about no food, right?

TEN MINUTES later, Jack had found the kitchen and opened every possible place to stash food. He found beer, cans of pop, and an open bag of chips. Judging by the sell-by date, the only possible course of action was to toss it into the trash, preferably wearing a hazmat suit. He'd also discovered that either Devlin hadn't fully moved in or he'd taken minimalist decor to the point of absurdity.

He'd have seen some sign before this if Devlin were subsisting solely on beer and pop. He might rely on takeout, but he'd also said to go to the guesthouse, which made no sense at all. The kitchen had a door that opened out on the back. In the hopes of getting a view of the lake, Jack opened the door. There had also been no sign of a pet, so he didn't worry about flinging the door wide open.

Yup. View of the lake, and direct access, but also, off to the right, near a thick stand of maple trees, was a small cottage. Guesthouse. The two buildings had been built in such a way that both houses would have an unimpeded view of the lake, but the guesthouse hadn't been visible at all from the front. In the dark, Jack had also missed the extension of the driveway, which appeared to loop around the house and lead right up to a single-car garage attached to the guesthouse.

His stomach grumbled, and Jack felt positively hollow. Fuck it. Devlin had told him to go to the guesthouse. Maybe he had some weird hang-up about cooking in his place? Maybe he was thinking of selling and… yeah, Jack didn't know what to make of it, but he was starving, and the guesthouse was a short walk away. If it was a bust, he'd drive somewhere. He was 80 percent sure he remembered the gate code to get back in.

Despite the bright sunlight, there was a slight chill in the air and a few orange and red leaves drifted across the beautifully manicured lawn, tiny reminders that winter was on its way. Wasn't cold enough to make Jack fetch his shoes. He was a hardy Canadian, chilly grass in the sunshine should be nothing on his bare feet.

He left the door unlocked behind him—the gate should keep things safe enough—and strode toward the guesthouse. The hanging planters made him pause, but his stomach goaded him on. He hadn't eaten hardly any dinner either, because Matt had made reservations at some molecular gastronomy place where half the things were foam and the other half were composed of weird little pearls. Interesting as a chemistry experiment, and tasty enough, but not exactly filling. The textures had also been a bit unappetizing. That wasn't the sort of place Devlin liked to eat, was it?

On that horrifying thought, Jack opened the door, stepped inside, and came to an abrupt stop. This was like the antithesis of the big house. Homey, but not kitschy or hopelessly outdated. No clutter, but from the foyer he could see a bookcase in the living room packed with well-loved paperback books. Devlin clearly spent his time here, not in the big house… except for maybe the bed, although he had a hard time picturing Devlin in this place. Why would he do that? The big house wasn't set up to be a showpiece, so it can't have had anything to do with impressing people.

Why wouldn't Devlin just move his bed in here if he preferred staying in a smaller house? He wanted to see what kind of books Devlin liked to read, but food first.

The kitchen was an easy matter to find, and Jack strode in.

"Hello?"

Jack's heart stopped. A woman sat at the kitchen table, doing a crossword puzzle and drinking coffee. He'd walked into someone's house, for fuck's sake. No hangover would be severe enough to prevent the diatribe Devlin had coming.

They stared at each other for what felt like an eternity, but it mustn't have been more than a second or two, otherwise she ought to be screaming or threatening to call the police.

"I'm so sorry," Jack croaked out. "Devlin told me to come over to find food. I must have misunderstood." Did this woman even know Devlin?

"Oh, that kid." Jack relaxed a fraction. She definitely knew Devlin. Jack was familiar with that brand of exasperation.

"I'm really sorry for just barging in. I'm Jack Johnson." Was it proper etiquette to introduce yourself to the owner of the house you'd just walked into unannounced? "I'll just be going." Obviously.

"I'm Beth, Devlin's mom."

Shock loosened Jack's jaw. "You are not." This woman was elegant, even in her kitchen, her blonde hair swept casually into a clip, but exactly perfect for a Sunday afternoon relaxing at home. And this was clearly Beth's home, not Devlin's. This woman fit perfectly into this decor.

She laughed, a merry tinkling sound that sounded very much like a feminine version of Devlin's. "Aren't you cute. I get that a lot. I was pretty young when Dev's dad knocked me up."

Jack gaped at her, and she laughed again. Dev was definitely related to this woman.

"Sorry if that was blunt." But she wasn't sorry. Anyone could see that. "I'd just turned eighteen when Dev was born, and his dad was nineteen. And as you can see, a life lived pure in thought does wonders for your skin." She winked at him, and Jack smiled.

"It was nice to meet you. I should go out and grab some groceries or something."

Beth rolled her eyes and headed to the coffee maker. "Jack, was it? Do sit down. Have a cup of coffee. I'll whip something up for the two of you."

"Oh, no, please. Don't go to any trouble." That wouldn't be too weird at all. But oddly enough, he accepted the cup of steaming coffee and let her guide him to a chair.

"Not to be rude or anything, but you don't look quite young enough to be one of Devlin's children."

Jack sputtered out a laugh. If he hadn't heard Devlin use that exact same description of his fellow students, Jack might wonder if Devlin had spent his formative years sowing bastards like dandelions.

"No, I'm not a student. I'm a friend." Saying he was one of Devlin's professors didn't sound fantastic either, so he left it at that.

"Ah. I assumed the unfamiliar car belonged to one of his new friends from the card club. Dev mentioned he might even host a tournament at his place, since there's plenty of room."

A reasonable assumption. Maybe. Jack was tempted to ask how many times Beth saw unfamiliar cars at the big house. And how many guys Devlin had sent over to get breakfast. For all she knew, he was, well, a one-night stand. Taking a walk of shame in front of Devlin's mother was pretty harsh, and just the appearance was bad enough. Jack hadn't even combed his hair. It probably looked like a wild ebony bird nest. He'd made no attempt to look like he hadn't just gotten out of bed, because it never occurred to him that he'd meet anyone else.

Instead of asking probing questions like a jealous lover, Jack sipped at his coffee. Beth started pulling things out of the cupboard and fridge.

"Are you vegan? Gluten-free? Any allergies?"

Jack blinked at her. "Uh. No, to all of it. But really, the coffee's plenty."

Beth tsked at him. Was this how mothers acted around their adult children's friends? Jack's memories of his own mother were overshadowed by the demands his father made to take up sports, to focus on manly things. He remembered his mother taking care of him a few times when he was sick but had no real memory of being "mothered."

"It's no trouble. And pancakes will keep in the oven until Devlin drags himself out of bed." She cracked a couple of eggs into a bowl before she paused and stared at him.

All the merriment had left her expression, and she chewed on her lip as though considering what to say. "How is he? Um… yesterday would have been hard for him."

Jack's heart skipped a beat. Of course his mom would know that and be concerned, but Devlin probably didn't want to discuss Trent with her any more than he wanted to talk to the rest of the band.

"It was, yeah. But… he survived it."

Her lip trembled, just a bit, before she nodded and turned back to the bowl of ingredients. Devlin didn't strike him as suicidal, but maybe moms tended to imagine the worst.

While she measured and stirred—Jack didn't think he'd ever had homemade pancakes before—Jack sipped at his coffee. Beth had to have so many answers, but should he ask? Would she tell him?

There was one question that needed to be answered, and he didn't know if Devlin would tell him the truth.

"Were Devlin and Trent… together?"

Her mouth twitched up in a halfhearted smile. “No. And Trent was straight. Unrelentingly straight.”

Interesting, since Devlin was unrelentingly gay. “There are an alarming number of gay men who’ve fallen in love with straight guys.”

This time she flashed him a wicked smile. “Just six beers to go from straight to gay.”

Jack choked on his coffee at the unexpected joke, based on the ridiculous urban legend that the only difference between a gay man and a straight man was six beers.

“Honestly, though, I never saw anything like that. Dev loved Trent, but like a brother, not a boyfriend.” She sniffed and wiped at her eyes before she continued mixing arcane ingredients.

“I’m sorry for your loss.” She’d known Trent every bit as long as Devlin had, even if she hadn’t spent as much time with him. Jack could admit to being relieved Devlin hadn’t been in love with Trent. Any thoughts of getting closer would’ve had to be put on hold if that were the case. Not that Jack was having thoughts… that he wanted to think about while hanging out with Devlin’s mother.

“Thank you.” She put the heat on under a griddle and poured herself another cup of coffee before turning around, resting her back against the counter. “When his dad died, he drank too much. Trent shook him out of it, but he took it hard. I’ve been worried.”

Jack sighed. “I see him a couple of times a week, and I haven’t seen any signs of an alcohol problem. Last night, yeah, he got pretty wasted. I was worried about him and got him home.”

“Would you recognize an alcohol problem? They can be sneaky about it sometimes.”

“Sounds like you’ve had personal experience.”

She nodded. “Yes. My sister.”

“My dad. Not when I was young, but later.” And there was literature about it at work. He didn’t think being starstruck would blind him to the signs in Devlin.

“Well, that eases my mind some.” Beth turned back to the pancake mix and poured batter onto the hot griddle. The scent was heavenly, and it didn't look too hard. Jack did a bit of cooking for himself but pancakes had seemed unnecessarily luxurious. He might have to try it sometime.

He had a sudden flash of Devlin in his apartment, in his bed, and Jack bringing him pancakes. He almost snorted aloud. That wouldn't make Devlin too spoiled. Beth clearly had cornered the market on that.

"What's the deal with Luke and Mo?"

"Oh, that kid of mine." Beth flipped the pancakes. "He's stubborn. So stubborn. And he doesn't deal well with loss, as I said. He's got some idea in his head that close friends who knew Trent will make it harder to deal with. Too many reminders. So he pushed them all away."

Jack had never had to deal with a death like this, but that didn't sound like a healthy response. Not if he was going to get past the grief.

"Do you talk to them?"

"Of course. We chat on the phone. Not that I tell him that. Trent, obviously, was almost like a second son. But the other two? Also like my kids. Mo's dads are on one of my charity committees, and we have lunch sometimes. Luke's mom taught Dev piano for a couple of years, so Luke comes by that talent honestly. We go out for coffee. Their music… well, if you're not used to it, it might sound harsh, violent, rebellious. In some ways it is, but they weren't in it to rebel. Greg, Devlin's dad, used to call them his little social justice warriors. Annoyed them to no end, but most of their lyrics do speak to politics and societal issues. Don't dismiss it because it's not something you're used to."

Devlin was an idiot. He had a huge support network if he'd just make use of it. He didn't mention to Beth he knew and loved Negative Impression. At some point he'd have to fess up to Devlin about that, and it might be better than him finding out from his mom first.

"No. Of course not."

While they chatted, Beth put a giant stack of pancakes on a cookie sheet and slid it in the oven to keep warm, while divvying up the rest unevenly on two plates, giving Jack the lion's share. She upended a bottle of pure maple syrup over his pancakes, yet another luxury he'd been unaccustomed to growing up.

If he'd had control over the bottle, he'd have drizzled lightly, but Beth seemed to know he actually preferred pancakes that were soaked.

He took a bite. "Oh, Beth, these are delicious." He was ruined, absolutely ruined for toaster waffles.

"Thanks." Beth took a modest bite from her pancakes.

"I've never had anyone make me pancakes."

Beth paused in her chewing and gave him a hard look. "They're not hard."

He smiled. "I was thinking that. Maybe I'll have to try it out sometime."

"Cooking from scratch is a bit of a luxury for me." There was a weight to her words that made Jack listen closely, even though he didn't know what point she was trying to make. "I mentioned how young I was when I had Dev? Greg and I married days after my eighteenth birthday, and I basically carried a beach ball up the aisle under my dress, because I was eight months pregnant. Greg was in first year at university, I was heading there in the fall, but having a baby changed everything. We both had to cut school back to part-time, get jobs, find childcare, scramble for grants and scholarships and financial aid. My parents never forgave us. Greg didn't reconcile with his parents until Devlin was in high school."

Jack had no idea why she decided to give him all this personal background, but he ate his pancakes and listened. It fed a long denied part of him that wanted to know everything about Devlin Waters.

He nodded, hoping to keep her talking after she took another bite and chewed.

"In those early years, we were dirt poor. Like, 'going to the food bank' poor. Like 'boxed pasta and dented cans of soup' poor. I don't know what we would have done in this day and age because Devlin took a peanut butter sandwich to school every day—no name-brand peanut butter, and it gave a lot of bang for the buck. Eventually, things got better. I learned how to cook from scratch because… that orange cheese in the boxes of mac and cheese." She shook her head. "But let me tell you, Dev loved that stuff. I don't know if they still make it, because it's in one of the many aisles I avoid at the supermarket, but that orange powdered cheese used to come in a bottle with a shaker. It was cheaper than parmesan, by far, even the parmesan powder that comes in a shaker. They'd sit on the shelf, side by side, one container blue and one container green. And every time, I'd grab the blue container with the electric orange powder. I'd shake some extra into the mac and cheese to give it a kick. I'd put it on Dev's spaghetti and meatballs."

"Uh. What? Like with tomato sauce?" Jack wrinkled his nose as Beth laughed. "Yup. His dad and I chose to go without. Anyway, my point is… this house, the money… it's not something he's particularly used to, even now. There are certain things that are easier for him because of it, sure. But half my committees are made of wealthy people who've never known anything but wealth, and they have a different outlook. It's hard to find common ground. Aside from the band, Dev has never had an easy time connecting with people. Partly because he doesn't understand a rich person's outlook, and partly because people who have average incomes assume he can't possibly understand them."

Oh. Jesus. Were all moms able to see right through people like they were psychic?

"More coffee?" Beth offered like she hadn't just reached into Jack's mind and read him as easily as picking up a book.

"Uh. Sure. Thanks."

Beth used the last of the pot to freshen his coffee and went about making a new pot. He hoped that wasn't for him, or he was going to float out of here on a river of caffeine.

"How long have you known Dev?"

Jack stuffed a giant forkful of pancakes in his mouth while he considered his answer to that question. He'd been a fan of the band since he was thirteen. And he wasn't entirely sure he wanted Devlin or anyone of his acquaintance to know how much of his adolescent years had been spent fantasizing about… well… all the members of the band, but Blade most of all. Nope, that was information no one needed ever.

"Since the beginning of September." One month, but it had felt like so much longer. Nevertheless, he didn't want to give Beth an entirely false impression. "But he told me about Trent and the band just last night."

She looked thoughtful. "Thank you, Jack, for being there. He was determined to be alone. I've tried to tell him, that when my Greg died, having people around who share your pain make it easier, not harder, but he doesn't believe me. My friends were my lifeline. He doesn't understand how I got over it. And the truth is, I haven't. I don't know if I ever will. But there's a difference between healing and forgetting, a difference I'm not sure he's grasped."

Jack nodded thoughtfully and finished off the pancakes.

"Morning, Mom." Jack swiveled his head to the kitchen's entrance, where Devlin stood, looking as rough as Jack had ever seen him, but nevertheless kicked his pulse up a notch, in either fear or arousal. Or both.

"Morning, kid. Rough night?"

Devlin let out a strangled sound, then coughed. "Yeah. Kinda."

"There are pancakes in the oven."

"Thanks, Mom." Devlin pulled the tray out of the oven, grabbed a plate, shifted the pancakes, then turned toward the table. And froze, his eyes bleary, bloodshot, and opening wider than Jack would have thought possible.

Surprises all around this morning.

"Er. Hi. Jack."

DEVLIN WAS too fucking old for this kind of hangover. He definitely didn't bounce back as quickly as he used to. He thought he'd learned his lesson after his dad died, but apparently not. All that booze had seemed like a good idea last night.

He'd dreamed of Jack. Dreamed of holding him close, breathing in the scent of his skin. And somehow, there was a memory of him crying, jumbled up with hugging Jack. The dreams were vivid enough that his pillows even smelled sort of like Jack. But not quite familiar at the same time. For a moment when he'd awoken, he thought he'd actually slept with Jack. He had a memory of being turned on and stroking his dick, but if he'd had sex, he didn't recall. He assumed he didn't because that was the sort of thing he remembered.

Once he'd dragged himself out of bed, drank some water, taken something for his head, and determined he wasn't going to have to pray to the porcelain god, he'd stared around his bedroom, unable to shake the idea that maybe Jack had been there. Aside from a stray pair of socks that Devlin couldn't definitively identify as not his own, there wasn't a trace.

It had been a good dream, but he needed to shake it off.

As he'd done so many weekends lately, he wandered downstairs, out the kitchen door, and into his mother's place. The only real surprise is that he didn't crash on her couch last night. But then he wasn't entirely sure how he got home, so maybe he'd had the sense not to wake her up with his drunken fumbling.

Pancakes and sympathy. He didn't want to talk about Trent—he'd already done plenty of wallowing—but his mom knew how hard yesterday had been for him.

Then he turned, and there was Jack. The corner of his lips glistened with a stray drop of maple syrup and his hair was a tousled sexy mess. He dropped his gaze to his grass-stained bare feet, much like Devlin's own, except Jack's feet were somehow attractive.

Arousal surged through him, and then other memories from the previous night became clear. He'd talked—a lot. He'd cried—a lot. He'd unloaded a giant vat of emotional baggage on Jack in a manner he'd never have done if he'd been sober. And that was around a number of fuzzy patches, where he didn't recall what happened. Shame swamped most of his joy at seeing Jack, mostly because… it was too weird. He couldn't even remember if they'd had sex, dammit. How did he ask that? Jack had slowly become less prickly over the past weeks. If he stepped wrong here, he'd regrow new armor with fresh quills.

"What are you doing here?"

Jesus fucking Christ he was a moron. The way Jack's back stiffened would have told him that, even if just hearing his words hadn't been enough. But he couldn't call them back. Didn't know how to apologize. Wasn't sure he liked knowing Jack had seen him at one of his lowest points. Not exactly impressive or attractive.

"I was chatting with your new friend, Jack," his mother said in a warning tone. He didn't need scolding from her either. And why did he want to call Jack JJ?

"Oh? And you just go wandering into random houses?" Fuckity fuck. Devlin nearly clapped a hand over his mouth. He couldn't seem to stop. Was he still fucking drunk?

"Actually, you told me to come here. In fact, your exact words were: No food in the kitchen. Go to the guesthouse. Of course, you failed to tell me I'd be walking in on your mother."

"Uh. I did?"

"Yes. You wouldn't let me out of bed until I promised I'd get something to eat here."

Bright pink spots flared to life on Jack's cheeks as he realized what he'd said, and they both twisted to stare at Devlin's mom, unable to say anything. He shouldn't be embarrassed about his sex life, dammit, he was forty-one. But it still felt a little like that time his mom had walked into his room when he was supposed to have been studying with Gordon Knightsbridge.

"Okay, kids, that might be my cue to leave. Shopping, then I'm heading to a girls' dinner. Jack, I trust I'll see you soon."

Well that hadn't been too obvious. She definitely expected Devlin to fix this, to the point that Jack would come back. Jack was his fucking professor. And he was horrified he couldn't remember having sex with him. Because he'd wanted it so bad, and it sucked he couldn't remember anything but kissing the back of his neck.

They stayed frozen, not speaking, until his mom grabbed her purse and sailed out the door.

"Did we?" Better to know than not, and if it did, he'd apologize.

Jack turned a ferocious glare on him. "Nothing happened."

"But you said…."

"I slept in your bed, yes. I was worried about you. And you seemed to, uh, like cuddling. You just didn't want me to leave, but you were mostly asleep. I think. But nothing happened."

"I woke up naked."

Jack threw his arms up in the air. "That's because you never… I mean… you were going commando."

Devlin frowned. "But you undressed me."

"Oh for fuck's sake. Your clothes are tight enough I was worried you'd cut off circulation or something. You might have been naked, but I wasn't."

Shit. His headache, which had been merely a background annoyance, awoke, throbbing and painful, from the excess emotion and volume.

"I'm sorry." He lowered his voice and rubbed his temple.

Jack's nostrils flared. "For what?" Those two words dropped the temperature in the room to near freezing.

"For getting so drunk you needed to bring me home. For… dumping all sorts of emotional crap on you. For… did I kiss you? I think I kissed you. On your neck. And you smelled good."

Jack's fierce flush remained. "Yes. You did."

"I'm not apologizing for that."

"You don't need to apologize for the other things."

But something was wrong, and he didn't know what. Jack was jumpy and out of sorts, and it could only be something Devlin had done.

Jack rolled his eyes. "Just sit the fuck down and eat your pancakes. They're awesome."

Stomach roiling, he sat and didn't argue, but he only picked at the pancakes.

Slowly the mood smoothed out, his headache subsided to background noise, and Jack brought him a cup of coffee.

"Thank you." Devlin smiled at Jack.

"I wanted to talk to you about the band."

Devlin's whole body tensed. No one could let it alone, could they? "I know what you're going to say." He stabbed his fork into his pancakes and twisted them apart.

"I doubt that. I wanted to say—"

"No!" The word exploded between them, and his headache pulsed angrily behind his eyes. "I know what my mother wants. I know what Luke and Mo want. The band is done, over in all but the paperwork."

Jack flinched back in his seat like Devlin had hit him. "But you're a talented musician. A successful one. I don't know why you're searching for a different career at all."

No, no, no. He'd endured all the feeling he could handle last night, and even that he hadn't been able to deal with sober.

"Everything about that band reminds me of Trent. We wrote all the music together. We purchased equipment together. One of the practice guitars is the same one we purchased by working at Canada's Wonderland during the summer."

"Those are good memories, Devlin. Valuable. You should be hoarding those memories, not shutting them away. Every song must be a whole book's worth of memories, between writing, composing, and performing. Playing them again should keep Trent with you."

Jack heedlessly ripped away those bandages inside, exposing the void within, uncaring of the pain. What the hell had he told Jack last night? How did he know all this?

"Don't you understand? Negative Impression was like magic. But it's broken now. The music in my soul is dead and gone. It can't be recreated."

And the wound it left behind continued to bleed.

"But…."

"No one, not you or my mother or the rest of the band, is going to convince me to just try again. I don't ever want to hear, much less play, a Negative Impression song again. And I'm forty-one years old. If I don't find something else to do with my life, I'm going to rot in that big house, on a steady diet of streaming movies, until the day I fucking die."

Devlin stared down at his plate, poking at his pancakes, until Jack finally put them both out of their misery. With a scrape along the floor, Jack pushed his chair away from the table. "I'll just see myself out. I'll… see you in class."

For a moment Devlin considered dropping out. Of all his classes. Not just archaeology. But that was the hurt and anger talking. He hadn't been lying. He desperately needed new purpose in his life that didn't involve music.

He stared at the mess on his plate while another hot wash of tears slid down his cheeks. He was finally alone, and it was the worst thing in the world.

WEDNESDAY AFTERNOON, Jack slumped at his desk, head in his hands. He ought to be grabbing lunch before his office hours, but he couldn't eat. Sunday night, he'd lain awake in the dark, going over every pain-laced word Devlin had thrown at him. Monday was Thanksgiving, and although he'd gone through the motions—visiting his dad in the morning, having dinner at Stephanie and Ian's—all he could think about was Devlin. Normally Thanksgiving made a nice break in the fall semester, but he'd have much rather been in class, seen for himself if Devlin was doing okay. Unfortunately he hadn't handled the situation well at all, and he had no way to rectify it, or even apologize.

He thought he'd gotten past that horrible one-night stand, but something about Devlin's reactions when he found Jack with his mother had been too glaringly reminiscent of his dismissive manner after they'd had sex. Then there'd been that brief moment—accompanied by a flare of anger—when Jack had thought Devlin remembered him and was apologizing for that.

His own emotional baggage had blinded him to Devlin's, and Jack's ire was a petty and selfish thing in comparison to what Devlin was going through. If Jack truly intended to be his friend, then he needed to keep Devlin's feelings in mind.

He'd also tried to tell Devlin… about his love of Negative Impression or maybe the existence of Crimson Corrosion. But Devlin hadn't let him finish, and what Devlin said about Negative Impression basically meant Jack couldn't ever really say anything about it. Maybe in a few months, or a year, he'd be in a better frame of mind. It would simply have to remain a secret until then. But Devlin excising music out of his life completely? No wonder his mother and bandmates were worried about him.

Jack had been a dick—an utter dick—and his behavior had kept him awake and gnawed at him ever since. Devlin had been mad, angry like a cornered dog, ready to bite any approaching hand, and much of that had been Jack's fault.

Last night he'd given up on sleep about three in the morning and thought about listening to a marathon of Negative Impression tracks but felt almost like he'd be betraying Devlin by doing so. Instead, he put on *Love Actually*—he didn't care it was only October—and tried to pretend that happy endings were possible.

The hours dragged until Wednesday's 9:00 a.m. Intro to Archaeology class. Jack arrived early, anxiousness giving him the energy to fake alertness. When he realized, finally, that Devlin hadn't come to class and didn't seem likely to, his stomach flipped, nausea weakening his knees. Somehow he'd finished the lecture, but he had no idea if he'd been at all coherent. Neither Sanji nor Meredith looked panicked or tried to interrupt, so Jack must have muddled through okay.

He couldn't even lock himself in his office and fret. He had another three hours of classes before he got a break. The wheels at the registrar's office ground slowly. It might be weeks before he got official confirmation that Devlin had dropped out of his class. All Jack had was his address and maybe the code to the gate, although he couldn't swear that he remembered it. He didn't have a phone number or an email address through which he could beg and plead for forgiveness.

He might be reduced to writing a letter, but who even paid attention to mail these days? All of Jack's bills came via email and were paid automatically out of his account. His mail was full of garbage that he barely glanced through before he dumped it in his shredder. No reason to think Devlin would be different. Even worse, what if Devlin had some sort of assistant who went through his mail? Jack hadn't seen any sign of such a person, but then neither had he seen a great big pile of *mail* in his unofficial tour of Devlin's house.

Fucking hell. Showing up at Devlin's front door equaled stalker-like behavior, and he suspected anyone in the music industry planned for unwelcome people who didn't respect privacy.

A hesitant knock at his door startled him. He rarely kept his door closed, unless he had work that needed serious concentration. Today, though, he didn't want random students to walk by and see his agitation. He scrubbed at his face, hoping he didn't look like he'd been on a weekend-long bender.

"Come in."

Devlin slipped inside and shut the door behind him. For a split second, Jack wondered if he'd fallen asleep and was dreaming.

But then Devlin walked closer, and something was off. Devlin hadn't thrown himself casually in the chair, slinging a leg over the arm. Devlin at rest was all curves and sinuous waves, and that's how Jack would dream of him. This Devlin was all jangled nerves and stiff, awkward angles. Jack's Devlin stared people defiantly in the face, daring them to do… whatever. This Devlin stared at the ground. He was barely recognizable.

Jack stood and rounded his desk. "Devlin, please, I'm so sorry. I shouldn't have said those things to you."

That, at least, got Devlin to look up. His eyes were almost as bloodshot as they'd been when Jack had left his house. The almost overwhelming urge to hug him welled up in Jack, but he couldn't. He didn't dare.

"I'm sorry too. I… said a lot of things I shouldn't have. I didn't mean… I didn't want you to go. But thank you. Thank you for being my friend."

Friends. He'd thought friends would work, but now he wasn't sure it would be good enough. He didn't have much choice in the matter, though.

"Thank you for letting me be your friend."

"And I'm also sorry about Matt."

"Matt?"

"Yeah, he… I think I remember him being pissed off?"

Jack shrugged. "Don't worry about that. It wasn't going anywhere with him."

Devlin heaved in a deep breath. "So…."

"Don't do it." Jack just knew what Devlin had come in person to say.

"Don't?" His voice sounded even smaller than before, and a diminished Devlin made the world a darker place.

"Don't drop out of the class. Please. Stick it out. You've… I know what I said about your music, but I can also see you'd do well at… just about anything this university can offer. Stay, please, and find your next passion."

Devlin let out a little bleat of surprised laughter. "Uh. I was going to ask if you wanted to go for lunch."

Jack squinted at him as though that would help him make sense of Devlin's words. "Lunch?"

"Yeah. My treat. As an apology. I'm not dropping out." Devlin carded his fingers through his hair, looking abashed. "I just… haven't been sleeping well and slept through my alarm this morning."

Relief, and the realization that he was starving, made Jack a little shaky.

"I can do lunch. As friends." Because Jack needed that clarification. This couldn't be a date.

"As friends."

Jack refused to be disappointed by getting what he said he wanted. Just like he refused to spend any time remembering Devlin's sleek, tattooed form as he stroked his cock. Nope. Not going there.

"What were you thinking?" Jack was hungry enough to eat just about anything.

"Salad King?"

"Oh yeah. I haven't had Thai in a long time, and I love that place."

"Let's go. You've got to be back for office hours." Devlin winked, but the shadows under his eyes served as a reminder that he wasn't as cocky and insolent as he often appeared.

ONCE THEY were seated at the communal stainless steel tables, along with an eclectic mix of patrons, and steaming plates of pad thai in front of them, Jack finally let go of the tension that had kept him wired for the past twenty-four hours.

Devlin closed his eyes as he savored his first bite, and Jack took the opportunity to inspect him. The man looked exhausted, and no wonder. He'd probably been holding that emotional firestorm in for months, and the weekend had taken its toll. Despite Devlin's defensive words in Beth's kitchen, Jack hoped he'd turned a corner, but Jack wasn't about to test the theory out by talking about anything Negative Impression-related.

Then Devlin licked his lips and let out a breathy little moan, and Jack forced his gaze back to his plate before he got hard in one of his favorite restaurants.

"You know, we used to come here back when we first started getting paying gigs. It's not too far from a lot of the dives we used to play in." Devlin sounded bemused.

Jack didn't want to draw attention to the fact that Devlin was starting to talk about the band on his own. It seemed like a good sign, though.

"Oh yeah?"

"Mmhmm. Remember before the renovations when it looked sort of like an old-time cafeteria? Orange vinyl and a menu made up of plastic letters on some sort of pegboard. With that PA system that was supposed to call out order numbers but mostly sounded like Charlie Brown's parents. The food, though—always awesome."

Jack grinned. "No, I don't remember that at all. I didn't start coming here until it looked like this. Don't forget, you're older than I am."

Devlin glared at him. "I'm not that much older. Am I? How old are you anyway?"

"Thirty-four."

"See? Only seven years apart."

"Uh, yup. Not many." Shit, shit, shit. Jack had nearly fucked that up. Because he knew damn well there were only seven years between them. He'd known that for a long fucking time.

"I can't believe you never came to the old place."

"Nope. When I was in university as a student, I heard people talking about Salad King, but I couldn't figure out why a place that sold salad was so damned popular."

Devlin snort-laughed. "Ha, yes the name is a little misleading, isn't it?"

The conversation flowed easily from there, and Jack was grateful for Beth's insight. There might be a significant disparity in their incomes, but Devlin truly wasn't pretentious, and he found the appeal in things that fit well within Jack's budget. He also wasn't… an asshole. At least, not full-time.

This might not be a date, but it felt a lot closer than any of the three evenings he'd spent with Matt.

CHAPTER NINE

ON A Wednesday around a month after Trent's birthday and the meltdown that had somehow altered Devlin's taunting flirtation with Jack to a friendship fraught with sexual tension—at least on Devlin's side—Devlin sat in the lecture hall, waiting for Jack to arrive. They'd seen each other almost every weekday since, somewhere out of class, whether it was for office hours or grabbing a bite. Jack had been great about respecting the boundaries Devlin had set about Negative Impression, but after having opened the floodgates, he occasionally let an anecdote or two slip out. They didn't hurt as much as he'd thought, but Jack never probed further, for which Devlin was grateful.

Their friendship was great, but he wanted to push for something more date-like, a movie maybe, or dinner at a decent restaurant, but patience had gotten him this far.

Nevertheless, it was maybe time to remind the professor that he wanted to be more than friends. Jack had been in his bed once, and Devlin wanted him back there, and not simply to provide comfort.

For the past few weeks, he'd been pretty good in class, letting Jack off the hook, but now that they were on more solid footing as friends, it was maybe time to start teasing again. Devlin had found this ridiculous fat pink pen. Probably they hadn't realized just how much it resembled a dildo made of bubblegum, but he had faith that if he put that up to his lips, maybe gave it a tiny lick or kiss, Jack would see the resemblance immediately.

It was almost December… maybe Santa would bring him what he wanted this year. His mom had already hinted she wouldn't mind a guest for Christmas dinner.

When Jack finally strode in, after the last student straggler, he walked right to the lectern but didn't glance at Devlin, which was a little odd. Jack had a thing about discretion, especially in front of the entire class, but usually Devlin got at least a little quirk of the lips. Most of the students, including Ken, who Devlin saw in archaeology and twice a week when he showed up at Excalibur, were completely oblivious to Devlin and Jack's deepening friendship. Discretion had been well served.

Devlin leaned forward, pen poised near his lips, eager for Jack's first glance his way. Hopefully it would be in the middle of a sentence. That tiny pause where Jack froze and stared, then picked up his thoughts as soon as his gaze left Devlin made him shiver. Playing was so much fun, but he was starting to feel like they'd had weeks of foreplay, and Devlin was dying to get to the naked bits. He was wearing Jack and his propriety down, he could tell.

"Before we begin, I have an announcement. Dr. Redmond is returning from maternity leave. This will be my last lecture for this class." The collective gasp from the students behind him covered his own. He couldn't quite imagine another person in front of this class. Devlin gripped his brand-new pen so tightly his knuckles whitened.

For a man who'd spent about a third of his life touring from city to city, country to country, he'd recently discovered a fresh new loathing of change. Not hard to trace the source of that development, but seeking a new career, trying to live life with all new friends, and actively pursuing a new man hit his change-o-meter limit. This alteration in a schedule he'd internalized and come to rely on felt like another loss, tiny in the grand scheme of things but a loss nonetheless. He should have been prepared; he'd known, in an abstract way, that this was coming.

A vein throbbed in his temple, and his breathing sped up.

"Dr. Redmond is an excellent professor. You'll all do quite well. The syllabus won't change. Due dates won't change. The schedule was set by Dr. Redmond. I was merely implementing it, so don't think you can use that as an excuse."

Despite his unease with this announcement—Jack hadn't mentioned anything about it at lunch yesterday—Devlin had to grin at his stern professor. He really did kinda get off on that, and it seemed a bit kinkier since Jack was younger. Not much. Plenty old enough for activities Devlin had in mind.

"As a little parting gift, and to give you some more time to get ready for exams, I'm canceling this week's lab sessions."

Devlin sat up straight. If it weren't for the cheering from the other students, he might have assumed he'd heard incorrectly. This was a "gift" Devlin wasn't much interested in. But Jack wasn't quite finished.

"My office hours will also be canceled for the rest of the week. If you have queries or concerns, please save them for next week. Dr. Redmond will provide specifics regarding her office hours during Monday's lecture."

Jack glanced his way for a brief moment, looking almost stricken, and Devlin wasn't sure how to interpret that expression. Was Jack warning him away? Why, exactly, had they never thought to exchange contact information? If they were friends, there was no reason they only had to interact during the week on campus.

Then again, he suspected Jack hadn't asked for any contact information because he was afraid. Afraid of crossing a boundary.

Devlin tapped his pen against his cheek. The distance Jack had been keeping between them… had that been solely because of their current professor/student roles? Devlin understood that under most circumstances there would be a power imbalance that could easily tip into harassment or coercion, but surely Devlin was an exception?

But maybe not. The faint stirrings of panic receded. This upset his schedule but might be the best thing to get himself out of the friend zone.

Jack proceeded to ignore him for the rest of the lecture. Devlin might not have forgiven him, except for the fact that he gripped the lectern for the entire hour as though it was the only thing keeping him from collapsing to the floor.

Devlin didn't bother listening to the lecture itself; he'd already read well past this in the text. He had plans to make, and as he considered a few ideas, he spent time imagining Jack naked. If only he hadn't been so drunk when he'd shared a bed with Jack. He remembered the feel of Jack's body in his arms and knew he'd been at least shirtless, but he had no recollection of what Jack looked like. If his plans worked, he'd be finding out well before Christmas, and maybe with enough regularity, he'd be able to give his mother an extra guest at the dinner table Christmas Day.

DEVLIN WAS losing his mind. Jack hadn't been kidding about canceling his office hours. He hadn't been in his office during his normal office hours Wednesday afternoon. The thought that Jack was actively avoiding him annoyed him thoroughly, and he'd taken that frustration out on some poor kids at Excalibur that night. Although he and the rest of Negative Impression had originally picked up on Magic: The Gathering as a way to pass the time on the tour bus and had spent years playing it, eventually the collectible nature of the game became too onerous for their nomadic life on tour, and they switched to other games, but mostly Dominion. When he'd joined a group about to play it, he was ready to spill a little blood—in the gaming world—and aimed for the most cutthroat strategies he'd discovered over the years.

Hardly fair to the rest of the table, but Ken had been ecstatic. Apparently he saw it as a good omen for the Dominion tournament the group was hosting Friday.

Thursday didn't improve his mood any. He'd tried swinging by Jack's office to have lunch with him—as they'd done a number of times since Trent's birthday—but Jack was nowhere to be found. Instead of studying, Devlin drowned his sorrows in cheesy rom-coms and pizza.

On Friday, when Jack again proved elusive at lunchtime, Devlin knew he needed another plan.

Devlin missed the prickly bastard, never mind getting him naked. And he was pissed that Jack thought just disappearing was an appropriate response to… whatever roadblock loomed in Jack's brain. Or even if it was simple panic because there *were* no more roadblocks.

The second Devlin finally cornered Jack, he was getting his fucking mobile number. He wasn't putting up with this again. Devlin had missed out on a potential thing once before, at a gig several years ago. Unfortunately, he'd been drunk enough to only have a fuzzy memory of his face, and aside from failing to get a number, he'd been an all-around dick for no good reason. Sure, he knew where Jack worked, but he didn't want to live with any more regrets.

After Devlin had lunch—by himself—he found an alcove with a good view of Jack's office, propped himself against the wall, and settled in to wait.

Of course Jack could have seen fit to leave early. It was a Friday, after all. But that didn't quite mesh with Jack's work ethic, and if Jack was avoiding him, he had to be as unsettled as Devlin was. Leaving early would only mean being at home with no distractions.

Except a phone and a dating app. Devlin narrowed his eyes. Matt was out of the picture; he wouldn't be pleased if Jack had been setting up dates.

Two hours later, during what would normally be their lab class, Jack slunk back into his office. Devlin nodded. This was better. Jack didn't have any further classes this afternoon. No excuses.

Devlin stalked down the hallway, urgency speeding his pace. He didn't want Jack to slip out again to head home. Not until they'd talked.

The office door was partially closed, but Devlin didn't let that stop him. He slipped inside and quietly shut it behind him. The sound of the lock flipping made Jack whirl around, hands to his chest like a Victorian maiden about to be compromised.

If Devlin was lucky, he'd be half-right.

"Devlin. What are you doing here?"

"Like you don't know." Devlin slunk closer, and Jack's hands fluttered.

Jack's cheeks went rosy. "I… well… I'm not teaching your class anymore… I assumed…."

Devlin rounded the desk, and Jack stepped backward until he met the wall. "Assumed what?"

"I don't know." But his cheeks got pinker. He knew. He just didn't want to admit it.

Devlin took another step closer. Their bodies didn't touch, but there was barely daylight between them.

"You're not my professor any longer. Did you think I only wanted to see you in a teaching capacity?"

Even Jack's mix of nonverbal responses bespoke his turmoil. Devlin hoped to God he'd interpreted this properly.

"No. Maybe. I don't know." Jack's voice was breathy, and Devlin had heard him like that before. He leaned in to nuzzle Jack's neck, careful not to touch him anywhere else.

"You smell so good." Devlin laid a light kiss on the vein that throbbed angrily in Jack's neck. Jack groaned.

"I can't do casual. I just… can't." Jack's voice cracked on the last word.

"Did I ask for casual?"

Jack's whole body stiffened, and he brought his hands up to push at Devlin's chest. Devlin stepped back. Jack's gaze snapped up, and Devlin met it without hesitation.

"What are you saying?"

"I don't want casual with you. I want serious with you."

Jack sucked in a breath, eyes glittering. "Dating and all that?"

"Dating and all that. But JJ…." Oh, yes. Judging by the flare of heat in Jack's eyes, Devlin hadn't misremembered giving Jack that name. "JJ, if you weren't aware, we've been dating for weeks. Lunches, conversation. Right here in this room."

Jack licked his lips. "We have?"

"Yes." Devlin cupped Jack's overheated cheeks with both hands and pressed their lips together. Jack shuddered, then opened up. Devlin pounced, devouring Jack's mouth with the insatiable hunger that had grown day by day since the start of classes.

He crowded Jack against the wall, then slid his hands down Jack's body, never giving up the fiery heat of Jack's mouth. Jack gave as good as he got, as hungry as Devlin was.

They'd been controlling themselves for weeks, but Devlin planned to gorge himself on Jack.

Jack wound his arms around Devlin's shoulders, tight, like he was worried Devlin would try to leave. Not a fucking chance.

Devlin squeezed Jack's ass with one hand, making Jack moan. Devlin was so fucking hard, and he could barely think about anything beyond the need to drop to his knees in front of Jack and suck his cock deep into his throat. Devlin slid a hand between them and pressed his palm against the hot, hard length of Jack's erection.

He was going to muss his fastidious professor up, but good.

Jack's kisses grew more frantic as he undulated against Devlin's cock massage. God. So fucking hot. If it weren't for his need to taste Jack's cock, he'd bet he could make Jack blow in his pants, just like this. The thought made his own cock jerk. If Jack blew a load in his pants, Devlin would be following quick behind.

Jack moaned into his mouth, and Devlin wanted to hear that sound unmuffled. He wanted to make Jack scream as he spurted in Devlin's mouth. The second he tugged on Jack's belt, though, everything stopped. Jack broke the kiss, panting.

"Not here," he gasped.

"What?"

Jack's hips slowed but didn't stop moving, rubbing his hardness against Devlin's hand.

"I… this is my job. I can't. Not here."

His dick clearly had other ideas, but Devlin understood. He hated it, but he understood. With a force of will he didn't know he possessed, Devlin took a large step back, taking his hands off Jack in the process. He hadn't realized how incendiary they'd been together, but without Jack in his arms, he was positively chilled.

"Come home with me tonight. Now. Or we can go to your place."

"Yes, oh God, yes."

Devlin shuddered at what he hoped was a preview of words he'd hear soon. Oh, so soon. Devlin sucked in air, trying to calm his racing pulse. They were doing this, and they were going to be serious about it. Christmas had come early.

Then Jack frowned. "Wait. Didn't you tell me you had a tournament tonight?"

"What?" Then he remembered. Excalibur. Dammit. He'd promised Ken. "Shit. I do."

"Tomorrow?" Jack's voice was still a sexy rasp, abrading his self-control.

"Yes. Come over early." Devlin kissed him. Briefly, although it was nearly painful to stop. "We'll spend Saturday and Sunday in bed."

Jack's breath hitched as he nodded.

Saturday. "Wait. Didn't you say you had plans with Stephanie on Saturday?"

Jack scowled. "Fucking hell. Yes. And she'll kill me if I cancel. I…. Devlin, shit. I can't cancel."

If Devlin weren't about to die of blue balls, he'd find this hilarious. They knew each other's schedules, and knew how important promises were to their friends. He snorted, and Jack's eyes narrowed.

"Something funny?"

"Yeah. Still think we weren't dating all this time?"

Jack's eyes widened, then he shook his head. "I guess… yeah, I guess we were."

Maybe the most chaste dating in the history of dating, but that was probably a good thing. He had a funny feeling Jack might have been less trusting if things had moved faster than glacial speed.

Then Jack smiled, and Devlin couldn't do anything else but smile back.

"I guess that leaves Sunday."

"Waiting might kill me."

Jack groaned. "Me too."

"Come over anytime. Early. Or I can go to your place?" As much as he wanted Jack in his bed, he had to admit the most enticing thing about his own house was how close his mom's place was, and he really, really hoped Sunday would be a mom-free day.

"You'd come to my place?" Jack sounded curiously hopeful.

"Of course I would. I'd love to see your place. You do remember I grew up poor, right? I'm not a snob. But you'd have to forgo my mom's pancakes."

Jack laughed a little. "Okay. Come to mine."

Devlin opened his mouth to tell Jack to text him the address when he remembered one issue he needed to rectify. "Give me your phone."

Jack wrinkled his forehead but handed it over. Devlin might not have ever considered dating Ken, but he'd learned one move from the kid.

Then he sighed. "Unlock it please." Ken had better moves than he'd realized. He'd done that little phone maneuver before Devlin's phone went to sleep and locked up, which meant he'd been paying more attention than Devlin had realized. Sneaky little brat.

At least Jack didn't ask why. Devlin used Jack's phone to call his. "Now you can text me your address."

"Slick."

With that half smile, Devlin could tell he was teasing, but he replied all the same. "I thought so. But it could use more practice."

Jack glared. "I think once was plenty. No need for practice."

Nope. No need. Devlin smiled. "See you Sunday."

"Sunday."

CHAPTER TEN

DEVLIN GOT out of the elevator and headed to Jack's apartment. Nerves tied his stomach in knots. He didn't know if he was too early or not. Jack hadn't answered his text, but Devlin had been pacing laps in his house, waiting for a reasonable hour. It was a reasonable hour. They'd have time for sex, followed by a late lunch, followed by more sex, then a nap…. After that, he was willing to play it by ear.

But Jack hadn't texted back.

He'd decided to start driving, because why not? He'd parked in visitor parking at Jack's building, but there was no text.

Mo and Luke had each texted him, though, so his phone wasn't broken, nor was he out of range. Sitting in the car hadn't done anything to calm his jitters. He got out and checked the intercom system. He'd been about to buzz up when a nice woman about his mother's age lurched through the door overloaded with groceries. He held the door open for her, helped her up to her apartment, and got a pinch on the cheek and was told he was a nice boy.

Then he grabbed the elevator and went up farther to Jack's floor. Now he stood outside the door, and he had no idea if Jack still wanted him there. For all Devlin knew, he wasn't even home, although Jack had replied Friday night when Dev texted highlights of the tournament. And he'd texted a couple of times Saturday, including his address.

Fuck it. Dev hadn't spent much of his life worrying things to death, and he wasn't going to start now, even though this might be one of the more important moments of his life.

He knocked on the door with a heavy hand and waited. Then he knocked again. Waited longer.

The deadbolt disengaged with a distinct *thunk*; then the door swung open. Jack's glossy black hair was flattened on one side, fluffy and wild on the other, like he'd showered before falling asleep with wet hair.

He had on a light blue long-sleeved pajama top and navy-striped, loose-fitting pajama bottoms. His cheeks were flushed with sleep, and he stood there, blinking.

"You look delectable." Devlin's voice was low and throaty. He wanted nothing more than to tumble Jack back into his warm bed and strip them both naked before curling up for a leisurely day of fucking and more fucking. He didn't know if fucking a boyfriend was different, but he was eager to find out.

Jack flushed and ran his fingers through his hair.

Like Devlin fucking cared. He pushed inside, took off his jacket, and hung it on a nearby hook before leaning in and pressing a kiss on Jack's neck.

"Uh. Sorry. I slept late." Jack shivered, and Dev kicked the door shut behind him. Then he bit down gently on that warm neck, like he'd been dreaming of.

"Oh fuck, Devlin," Jack breathed out the words.

He licked up the side of Jack's neck to his jaw, stubble prickling his tongue. Devlin would be happy to strip Jack naked right here in the foyer, but his joints might be past fucking on a cold, hard, tile floor.

"Want to show me your place?" He punctuated his question with another little bite, at the curve where shoulder became neck.

"Mmm. Oh. Yes."

Jack carefully stepped away, but his pajama bottoms were definitely not designed to disguise arousal. Devlin licked his lips in anticipation.

With a trembling finger, he pointed to the left. "Kitchen." He turned slightly and pointed at the open area in front of Devlin. "Living room and dining room. Balcony."

Then he turned back to the right and walked with determination down the hall. Devlin would follow that ass anywhere, and the little hip wiggle was all the invitation he needed.

As they walked down the hall, Jack pointed at doors. "Bathroom. Storage. Office." At the end of the hall was the destination they both cared about.

Devlin truly hadn't given Jack's apartment much thought, beyond recognizing he'd clearly spent some time making it reflect his personality. The bedroom, though, *that* he paid attention to. The walls were painted in a lush sand color highlighted with a glossy tan. The hanging lights were something straight out of Aladdin, and Devlin imagined at night they'd be utterly romantic, the geometric cut-out shapes spreading flickers and slices of lights all over the bed and walls. He'd seen lights like this in Morocco—they'd never played Morocco, but they'd taken a side trip to visit Casablanca after a show in Gibraltar.

The lush garnet drapes and matching bedspread were the perfect complement and looked like an ideal setting to fuck Jack into a puddle. Or vice versa.

"I love your place." Devlin wrapped his arms around Jack from behind, then ran his hands up and down Jack's chest while he bit and sucked at the flesh he could get to. But it wasn't nearly enough. It was like he'd been starving his whole life and he'd finally found the man who could satisfy him.

He slid Jack's top off. His sleep-warm skin smelled salty and male. Devlin coaxed him on the bed and watched Jack squirm on his back, hard cock tenting the pajama pants. Devlin stripped off his shirt, shoes, and socks. Jack stared intently as he flicked open the button on his jeans and groaned when he let them slide down his hips to pool on the floor.

Devlin hardly ever wore underwear, and his cock thrust out rampantly. Jack sat up, but Devlin didn't want that quite yet. He'd had dreams, and he wanted to let some of them play out now.

"Lie back."

Jack's forehead wrinkled slightly in an almost frown, but he followed Devlin's suggestion.

Devlin slowly peeled Jack's pajama bottoms down, revealing a mouthwatering cock, and he slid between Jack's legs to indulge one of his fantasies. He gently licked the tip of Jack's cock before opening his mouth and swallowing him whole.

Jack gasped and twisted his hips, like he wanted to thrust but didn't want to choke Devlin.

Devlin pulled off for just a moment. "Do it. Fuck my face."

It was a toss-up whether Jack's tortured moan was for Devlin's words or the way Jack thrust his cock deep into Devlin's throat. Hearing Jack's voice, normally so perfectly modulated and controlled, become gasping, harsh pleas interspersed with filthy fucking words made Devlin as hard as he'd ever been in his life.

Jack's hips undulated faster, and as much as he wanted to suck down everything Jack gave him, he didn't want their first time to end too quickly. Devlin's recovery time wasn't nearly what it used to be.

"Devlin," Jack moaned in protest when he lifted his head.

He kissed his way up Jack's belly, flicked a tongue over his nipples, then eased Jack onto his front. His eyes nearly rolled back in his head. Oh, that fucking ass was a thing of beauty. Sonnets should be written about it, sculptures should be made of it, however imperfectly they'd be able to duplicate it.

Drifting his fingers lightly over Jack's skin, he leaned over and licked along the bumps of his spine, drawing more shivers and stronger moans from Jack. He kissed the base of Jack's spine, teasing his crack, making Jack shift restlessly, legs spreading.

Devlin eased a hand between Jack's legs and coaxed his hips upward while cupping his hard cock.

Then he dove between Jack's cheeks and indulged in yet another filthy fantasy while Jack yelped and commanded and opened right the fuck up for him.

He didn't know how long he rimmed Jack, but everything was wet and messy when he finally lifted his head.

"Devlin, fuck me already."

Mmmm. He did like the orders, but he had other ideas. He moved back up over Jack's writhing body, his own cock slotting itself between Jack's saliva-slick cheeks.

"Did you want to fuck me?" Devlin asked.

Jack froze for a second, then twisted his head around, an incredulous look on his face. “You’d… want that?”

Devlin was too close to coming to argue stereotypes; hell, he could probably come all over Jack’s ass right now if he moved too vigorously. “Why wouldn’t I? I like getting fucked just as much as I like fucking.”

“Uh. Good to know.” Jack’s voice was strained. “But….”

Granted, he’d done prep as though he’d intended on topping, but every gay boy had to have a butt plug or two around.

“Got anything fun in your bedside drawer?”

Jack whimpered and buried his head in the pillow, ass still waving in invitation. “Knock yourself out.”

It was so hard to lift his cock out of the cradle of Jack’s ass, but Devlin did it, because if he didn’t, he just might plunge in completely bare, and that would make him a giant asshole.

In record time Devlin found exactly what he wanted. He quickly lubed himself up, then slid a gentle hand over Jack’s ass before lubing up a medium-sized plug and easing it home.

Jack moaned and shook. “Fuck. Devlin.”

Devlin shivered. That was the idea.

He helped Jack to his knees, slid a condom on that eager dick, then moved in front of him, spreading his ass in invitation while pressing his torso to the bed. A bit of a contortion but he kept himself in excellent shape.

“Fuck me.”

“Wha… prep?”

“I’m all ready.” Devlin was breathless with want.

Jack hesitated for no more than a second, and then the blunt head of his cock probed at Devlin’s entrance. There was a moment’s burn—and it burned just right—as Jack slid home, and they both groaned.

Then Jack dug his fingers into Devlin’s ass and thrust, hard and fast, just the way Devlin liked, pounding his gland. Desperate, he wrapped a hand around his cock and stroked in time with Jack’s thrusts. All too soon, his vision whited out, and he jerked and unloaded all over his fist. Behind him Jack shouted and squeezed his ass as he shuddered out his orgasm.

Devlin could barely keep from collapsing on the bed, but as vigorously as he liked getting fucked, he didn't like abrupt withdrawals. Jack curled over his sweaty back, panting, arms trembling as he struggled to avoid resting his entire weight on Devlin. Then he gripped the condom and slid out, as gently as Devlin could hope for.

With a sleepy smile, he watched as Jack walked gingerly to the bathroom. That butt plug would be making everything sensitive.

Soon enough Jack returned and slid into bed beside him. "Jesus."

"Hmm. I take it you've never done that before."

"Uh, no. It was awesome."

Devlin nodded. "Yeah, it's like getting fucked while you're fucking, but there's no distraction of a third party."

"Don't like threesomes?"

"No, not at all." Too many dicks, too many hands, too many distractions.

"Me neither." Jack smiled at him.

Good. Better to be on the same page.

"But we'll definitely be doing that again." Jack shivered.

"Uh, yes we will. Although next time, maybe we can play professor and naughty student."

Jack's eyes widened before he slapped Devlin's shoulder. "Seriously? That's what you were thinking every damned day in class, wasn't it?"

Fuck yeah. "Busted."

"Well, maybe I could be talked into that."

Fuck *yeah*. "After a nap, maybe."

Jack blinked sleepily at him. "You have the best ideas."

DEVLIN WANDERED into Jack's living room, more content than he'd been in months, and it wasn't simply the orgasms. He liked Jack. He had from the very first moment he'd been scolded by the man in front of four hundred students. In fact, signs were pointing to it being more than "like." But he'd never been in love before, and he sensed he needed to prove something to Jack. Or Jack was holding back. Not that Devlin had ever tried having a long-term relationship before, but it was the right time. There was nothing to be afraid of. This was the right man, and he was looking forward to learning all the things that made Jack the man he was.

He stopped at the bookcases. An oversize plush chair sat in the corner, flanked by two large bookcases. These were books for entertainment, because Jack had already shown him the study, aka the apartment's second bedroom. Jack had converted the room into a home office, and there was literally no wall space left due to the desk and bookcases. The shelves held mostly scientific, nonfiction books presumably related to archaeology, but there were also bits and pieces of pottery, beads, and carved tablets, and a shit-ton of paper. It was a room only an archaeology professor could love.

On the other hand, the living room was designed to be inviting for average nonarchaeologists, although Jack had hustled him through the tour pretty quick to end up in the bedroom.

A couple of shadow boxes decorated the walls, along with some abstract metalwork that had a real steampunk vibe. It was the reading nook that drew his attention first. It had nothing to do with Jack's work. Devlin peered at some titles on the upper shelf, recognizing them as crime thrillers, many of which he'd read, as they were a common staple in airport shops. There was a variety of books in different genres, all of which had well-worn spines indicating multiple reads.

The bottom shelf held romances, including a few gay romances. Devlin would have to tease him about them later, but then get Jack to let him know his favorite bits. Devlin wasn't against romance, not now that he had a boyfriend.

On the opposite side of the room, another bookcase was packed full of CDs. Devlin had a bigger collection, but after spending several evenings with the kids of Excalibur, it had become obvious that keeping hard copies of music collections wasn't common, unless one was into records. God, that had made Devlin feel fucking old. Records had been a medium on its way out when he'd started his musical career, and now it was retro and cool again. So weird. Since Jack was younger than Devlin, he was a little surprised he hadn't gone all digital. Then again, an archaeologist not only liked old things, they liked stuff in general. Stuff that pinged on visual and tactile senses. Maybe it wasn't all that much of a surprise.

He hadn't even realized Jack liked music all that much. Devlin bit his lip. He'd eased up on the moratorium on all things Trent, and had talked some about life on tour and early memories of him and Trent, but he hadn't been all that receptive to discussing actual music. His or anyone else's. All he knew was that the music at Ciao wasn't to Jack's taste. If he'd bothered to think about it, he'd probably have assumed Jack didn't care for music at all, but this enormous collection said otherwise. Emphatically.

Leaving the books behind, he headed for the music. For all that he couldn't feel the music inside anymore, it interested him more than books. He didn't mind reading, but he usually just picked up whatever had a decent title at the airport. He didn't follow authors or series with any sort of faithfulness. Not like he did with bands and musicians.

Jack's CDs were sorted alphabetically by artist. Devlin approved. Instead of skimming, he paid careful attention. They had a lot of bands in common. Devlin and the rest of the band had found inspiration from a wide variety of artists, new and old, but in terms of ones Devlin just liked to listen to? He and Jack had a lot more in common than he'd ever expected. Just went to show, couldn't judge books by the chinos they wore.

He kept going down the alphabet, more and more amazed at Jack's collection. Until he reached *N*. He checked, and double-checked. Every fucking Negative Impression release. Devlin frowned and pulled out a slimline jewel case in the middle that was too narrow to have anything on the spine.

What the fuck? The CD in his hand was a limited-edition promotional CD they'd given out during shows they played in the last three or four months in 1999, the two tracks on it inspired by the whole Y2K scare. This particular pressing was scarce. Sure, people could lay hands on it. Wasn't the crown jewels or anything. The songs on it weren't released on an album for another three years, but they were on an album, and a fan didn't need to lay hands on this particular piece of relatively pricey memorabilia in order to get them. Hell, all of Negative Impression's stuff was available from music-streaming services.

Something wasn't right. No matter how agitated it made him, it likely wasn't worth waking Jack up to ask him about it. Maybe he'd been able to buy a whole collection when Devlin told him the band name? That was an explanation that didn't set his teeth on edge. Nevertheless, Devlin held on to the promo CD so he'd have it at hand. As soon as Jack awoke, he'd ask.

A little jumpy, he moved on to the shadow boxes. One of them was a collage of concert ticket stubs, very artistically done. There were a lot, and some of the print was faded—Devlin needed to consider reading glasses soon, especially with all this studying—but he didn't look too closely, mostly because he was afraid he'd find Negative Impression ticket stubs in there. Was this a recent obsession? Or had Jack just… omitted telling him that he knew about the band before he'd met Devlin? The first made him wary—they'd had their share of obsessive fans over the years and had filed more restraining orders than he'd ever have expected when they'd first started out. The second felt a whole lot like a lie.

Tentatively he moved to the second shadow box. It contained a photocopied flyer on a sheet of that awful goldenrod-colored paper, artistically molded into a wavy, 3-D shape, and accompanied by detritus of a musical show at a club. Cardboard coaster, a cigarette butt, a couple beer bottle tops, and a guitar pick. Devlin squinted at the flyer behind the glass, a slight glare from the afternoon sun, his middle-aged eyes, and the weird shape making it difficult to read.

Crimson Corrosion featuring brand-new vocalist, Jack Johnson!

What the ever-loving fuck?

Definitely a band, since the flyer named four other people, each attributed to an instrument. The bottom had some sort of call to action and a diagonal banner, both of which were at a terrible angle to read. Devlin tilted his head and almost pressed his nose right up to the glass.

Featuring covers of Negative Impression!

Spots swam in front of his eyes, which somehow made the call to action more visible. Devlin had played in that same club in the early days of Negative Impression, but they'd soon outgrown the tiny venue. More importantly was the date of the show. Six years ago. Six fucking years ago. Devlin tossed the promo CD on the couch and pulled his phone out of his pocket.

Fuck, fuck, fuck. Well, now he knew what "plans" Jack had had yesterday. Yet another Crimson Corrosion show. With Jack singing. Singing Devlin's—Blade's—songs.

Devlin started pacing so he wouldn't rip the shadow boxes off the wall and toss CDs all over the room. Anger rippled under his skin. What was Jack's endgame? What had he truly thought to gain from this deception? There was no way Jack could manipulate the teaching schedules—he was 99 percent sure of that—otherwise Devlin would suspect this entire class and lab and office hours and all the shit was some sort of elaborate plan to get close to him.

Or what if… Jack had recognized either him or his name at the outset, and everything that followed arose merely from Jack taking advantage of an unexpected opportunity falling in his lap?

It made too much sense. Jack had been everything he'd thought he wanted, and now he had nothing again. He gasped against the phantom pain that threatened to rip out his heart. He'd never felt like this for a man, and maybe… maybe it wouldn't hurt so much if Trent's death hadn't left him so brittle. But on top of his already fragile state, this left his emotions flayed and left to soak in vinegar.

He'd… he'd been fooled by an unbalanced, obsessive fan. Jack had met his mother, been in his home. All the while perpetrating some elaborate scheme or prank.

Had any part of this "relationship" been real?

The burn of tears, all too familiar these past months, confirmed Dev's part had been real. He had to get out of here.

He had his phone and wallet in his jeans. His jacket, with keys, was by the front door. Shoes, socks, and shirt would all have to be sacrificed if he wanted to get out of here without going back in the bedroom and risk waking Jack. At least it hadn't snowed yet this season—a little cold he could deal with.

"Hey there. I was wondering where you'd gotten to."

Devlin whirled at Jack's words, partly startled, partly spoiling for a fight. Jack's eyes were sleepy, his hair tousled from Devlin's fingers, hickeys dotted his neck, and he leaned, indolent and completely gloriously nude against the entryway.

It wasn't right that Jack look so fucking gorgeous. Not when Devlin was so fucking angry with him. But he couldn't let Jack's appeal sway him.

"Were you? Because I was wondering when you were going to tell me about… oh… Crimson Corrosion. Or this."

Devlin picked up the promotional CD and tossed it across the room at the armchair. "What about the fact that you own every fucking goddamned CD my band has ever put out?"

Jack's face drained of all color, a feat Devlin might have marveled at any other time.

"Devlin, it's not what you think." He reached out a hand.

"No? Because it looks like you lied, every time I spoke about the band. And that either makes you a fucking psychopath or the shittiest motherfucker in the history of motherfucking. The prehistory of motherfucking, even." He was an archaeologist, after all.

A muscle flexed in Jack's jaw. "Do you think we can discuss this calmly?"

"Don't pull your professor bullshit on me. What was your plan? What did you hope to accomplish?"

Jack's blue eyes flashed, and the color returned to his cheeks in an angry rush. Devlin couldn't stop his visceral reaction because the image was so similar to the way Jack looked while fucking.

"Leaving my 'professor bullshit' aside—" Jack's voice could have flash frozen a side of beef while simultaneously carving it into ribbons. It might have mattered to Devlin if his heart wasn't already shredded. "—I was respecting your wishes."

"Are you shitting me? Are you really blaming me for your lies?" The anger was maybe over-the-top, but he needed the anger to keep the pain at bay. He'd bared his innermost thoughts for this man once already. He wasn't about to do it again.

"You said you wanted nothing to do with the band. You didn't want to talk about it. Fuck, you won't even return text messages from Luke and Mo… and they've been like your fucking family for over twenty years."

"That's different. And my relationship with Luke and Mo is none of your business."

"And you'd never let it be my business, would you? I wanted to tell you, and I planned to tell you."

Devlin sneered. "Easy to say now. When was this big revelation to take place?"

Jack's nostrils flared and he crossed his arms across his chest. "When I thought you could handle it. When I thought you wouldn't lose your goddamned mind over it. I didn't want this to hurt you."

"Too late." Devlin clamped his lips shut before he admitted anything else.

"Your attitude toward the band surprised me. I wasn't expecting so much pain in relation to the band, and I thought it better to wait. I'm sorry if I was wrong. This relationship is, like, three minutes old, and we haven't had time to get to know each other, not really. We haven't had time to build trust between us."

"You're fucking lying." Devlin didn't know why, but maybe it didn't matter. There had been too much time and too many opportunities, even before Devlin told him he wanted nothing to do with the band or the music. Fuck. Maybe he wanted some extra publicity for his stupid little cover band. "And what fucking relationship would that be? Because there's nothing here between us." Devlin clamped his mouth shut against the howl that wanted to escape.

"What? Devlin you can't be serious."

Devlin had no more words. If he opened his mouth again, he'd fall to his knees sobbing. How much more did the universe want to take from him? He stomped to the front door, Jack trailing him, talking, pleading, but Devlin shut his ears to it. He grabbed his jacket and walked out. Waiting for the elevator was out of the question, and he opened the door to the stairwell.

"Devlin, for fuck's sake, come back." Jack's shout was cut off by the heavy fire door slamming shut behind him.

The concrete was cold against his bare feet, and the satiny lining of his leather jacket was chilly and peculiar against his skin. If he went quickly, he'd be in the car and on his way before Jack found enough clothes to avoid getting arrested.

Devlin was an idiot to think he could somehow find love this late in his life.

CHAPTER ELEVEN

JACK RAN back into his apartment, yanked on the pajamas he'd been wearing when Devlin arrived, put on a pair of shoes, and grabbed his keys before racing down to the parking lot outside.

He put all his focus on getting to Devlin before he left, and none at all on assessing what had just happened. He could worry about that gaping wound if he couldn't catch up with Devlin.

Bursting out of the front door, he got outside in time to see Devlin's car roaring away. Jack's shoulders sagged, and he heaved in a ragged breath. He hadn't expected a sprint less than an hour after getting his brains fucked out. And then getting his heart fucked over in between.

After standing there a few moments, Jack had to admit Devlin wasn't coming back, and he went back up to his apartment, trying to remain calm.

His apartment seemed so empty without the vibrant presence of Devlin, who had—in Jack's mind—become someone other than the uncaring Blade. In a short span of time, Devlin had come to mean so much to Jack, and now.... Surely he hadn't meant it? He couldn't be gone for good, could he?

He obviously hadn't been thinking when he'd suggested Devlin come over. The CDs and the shadow boxes were pretty damning. But he hadn't been deliberately lying for some nefarious purpose, and so he'd never thought about hiding any "evidence." It hadn't once occurred to him.

Devlin had been so angry. Underneath that spiky shell of fury had been pain. So much pain, and it was precisely that pain Devlin carried around that made Jack take a second look. It made Jack want to heal him, want to never inflict any more hurt and yet... he had. Unintentionally, he had.

Chilled through to the bone, Jack stumbled back to bed and wrapped himself in a comforter.

With trembling fingers, he called Devlin.

Voicemail.

"Devlin, please call me. I'm sorry, but we can work this out. Let's talk."

Could they work it out? He wasn't sure. What if Devlin demanded a complete elimination of all things Negative Impression? Excising such a large part of Jack's life might not even be possible, even if Devlin was trying to do that exact thing.

Waiting in silence in the bed that still smelled of sex and Devlin—a scent he'd only just had a chance to wallow in—was too hard. He swiped a hand across his burning eyes and called Stephanie.

"What do you want? Need a break from your crazy sexfest?"

Jack drew in a shuddery breath. "Steph, I fucked up." Three days. He'd had a boyfriend all of three days and he'd fucked it up to the point…. "I think he dumped me." His voice cracked, and a stray tear dripped off his chin and hit his hand. Considering how cold he felt, the tear should have left a burn it was so hot in comparison.

"What?" Stephanie screeched. "Surely he's not that big an asshole."

"I don't know. Maybe I was the asshole this time."

"Impossible." In that moment, he'd never loved her more.

"Look, I haven't told you everything."

"You think?" She sounded offended. They did have a tendency to overshare, but much of what he'd learned about Devlin wasn't anything he could share without permission. Unless he was pond scum. Despite not having all the facts, Stephanie had been unsurprised that Jack's feelings about Devlin had changed. She maybe didn't know how far he'd fallen, though, considering just over two months ago he'd never thought he'd see Blade again and didn't think he'd piss on the guy if he was on fire.

Now, if he never saw Devlin again… he didn't want to contemplate the desolation he'd have to endure. Losing Blade four years ago would be nothing compared to losing Devlin.

Jack sighed. "Promise me this goes no further." He couldn't make this worse for Devlin, for both of them.

"You don't even have to ask."

He told her everything. Well, almost everything. There were certain details that Stephanie didn't need to understand.

By the time he was done, his voice was hoarse, and they'd both shed some tears, Jack more than Stephanie.

"What do I do, Steph? How do I fix this?"

He could almost hear her shrug. "I don't know. It's a pretty fucked-up situation. I think you might just have to wait it out. Keep trying to get in touch with him, but not so often he blocks you. Or, you know, you could just… let it go. Chalk it up to experience."

Jack thought about that for a fleeting second. The thought of getting back on one of those apps and meeting more men like Matt—who were perfectly nice but not perfect for him—was bleak. Utterly disheartening. No matter how awkwardly they'd started—since Devlin didn't even remember when they'd first met—Devlin suited him better than any other man he'd been involved with. And he knew now that he suited Devlin. It could have been a rock-solid relationship. It could have been a happy-ever-after if Jack hadn't fucked it up.

"This isn't all on you, you know."

"Of course it is."

"No. You did pretend you didn't know who he was, because you'd been hurt by the one-night stand that he didn't remember, and it colored your interactions with him. And he's overreacting. For a good reason—he's still grieving, it sounds like this is his first relationship, and he feels betrayed by you. He's having knee-jerk reactions all over the place, because his emotions are all out of whack. But unless he realizes it and decides to be reasonable and talk to you about this… well, you might not be able to fix this."

No. He couldn't accept that. There's no way their relationship could end like this.

Jack didn't have the energy or will to chat any longer, and he ended the call. He grabbed another blanket from the closet because he was fucking freezing. There wasn't any reason to get dressed, and he certainly couldn't choke down any food right now. As he turned back to the bed, he almost tripped over a small pile of clothes.

Devlin's red long-sleeved shirt, a pair of white athletic socks, and a pair of black Converse All Stars.

Fucking hell. Devlin had been in such a hurry to get away he'd driven home barefoot. He'd gone out into November weather without a shirt. If the guy ever wore underwear, they'd undoubtedly be in that small, sad pile too.

Jack picked up the shirt and clutched it to his face like a pathetic, lovelorn teen. He might not be a teen, but the other adjectives fit.

He took both shirt and extra blanket to bed, hoping he wasn't going to freeze to death before his alarm went off in the morning.

Somehow in mere weeks and three official days together, he'd started dreaming of supporting Devlin through his grief, figuring out how to mend the rift with Luke and Mo, learning to cook in Beth's kitchen, and harshest of all… waking up to Devlin's face every morning.

Maybe he'd started thinking too much too soon, but he wasn't mourning the loss of a three-day relationship. He was mourning the life he could have had, a life and a man he would have loved.

Tears slid, hot and stinging, down his cheek to wet his pillow.

DEVLIN'S TIRES squealed as he turned into his driveway. For a split second he was tempted to just ram the gate with his car, rather than wait for it to open automatically, but he wasn't a violent person, and he so rarely let his emotions get the better of him.

Fuck Dr. Jack anyway. He turned his phone off so he didn't see the glaring voicemail notification. He wasn't going to listen to it. There wasn't anything Jack could say to make this better.

He parked the car, then limped into the house. His big, empty, echoing house. Like his limbs were encased in concrete, it took time and effort to make his way up to his bedroom, where he shed his jeans and jacket. Slightly less encumbered, he turned on the shower, as hot as he could stand, and stood under the spray and let the tears come, the same way he'd done after finding Trent dead. The same way he'd done on all the days leading up to the funeral. The same way he'd done when his dad died.

Badass punk rockers didn't cry. They got tattoos and piercings or brawled, sublimating emotional pain in the physical. Sometimes they used sex as a balm. Or so he'd thought. When his dad died, that belief had been rocked. The uncomplicated sex he'd sought had left him with regrets. When Trent died, the foundations of that belief exploded into nothingness. If he'd thought there was a way to sublimate this pain with ink, he'd be covered in scribbles, head to toe. If sex made it better, he'd have been whoring himself on the street instead of waiting until he found a man who could be a partner, a husband.

Instead he learned to cry. But he didn't know how to let anyone see him. He didn't consider it a weakness for other men, only for himself, and he hadn't cried in the presence of another person since he was a kid. His mom was the last person to see him cry. Until Jack. Sure, he'd been drunk, but Jack had made him feel safe, and Devlin had broken down. Without the safety net he thought they'd been building together, he was maybe just broken. Irreparably.

Under the sheeting water, he tried to exorcise his pain, wrapping his arms around himself while he sobbed until his throat ached, his nose throbbed, and he could barely see out of swollen eyes.

Eventually there were no more tears, and he washed thoroughly. Bad enough there were a couple of bites to remind him of Jack. He couldn't bear the scent of their sex.

The cooling of the water told him he'd been in there long enough to exhaust his enormous water heater, and with arms like overcooked noodles, he turned off the water and stepped out of the shower.

Smears of blood marred the tiled floor. Exhausted and numb, he pulled first aid supplies out of the cabinet and sat on the toilet lid to doctor a foot he must have cut on something during his foolhardy escape from Jack's apartment.

Now that the emotional firestorm had eased, he could see that maybe he hadn't needed to leave Jack's place like the man had been threatening him with a machete.

Did Jack own a machete for when he went on digs? He'd have to ask…. Devlin cut that thought off with a gasp. No longer could he just bring random questions to Jack. No texting, no office hours, no listening to his melodic lectures. No hugs, no kisses, no inhaling his clean spicy scent that made Devlin want to dirty him right the fuck up.

Over. It was over and done. Like Negative Impression. No looking back.

He tensed his jaw against another emotional outburst, and he cleared his mind, focusing only on the task at hand.

After determining there was no glass in his foot, he cleansed it and bandaged it, then found himself back in the bedroom, in front of his computer. Almost before he realized it, he'd pulled up the university's web page detailing how to withdraw completely from classes.

Naked, he sat there for an indeterminate amount of time, trying not to think about archaeology without Dr. Jack, and not seeing him daily.

But the degree had been something for him. Trying to please his father had been part of it, sure, but somewhere inside, he'd known it was for himself. This was the only way he'd find a way to exist without music, and he couldn't let Jack take that away from him.

He still had a life to live, and even though he'd be doing it alone, he still needed a purpose to fill his hours.

A notification of more emails popped up. Probably Luke. Or Mo. Maybe both. He slammed the lid of his laptop shut. At least he didn't have to worry about homework or papers; he was all caught up, and the papers that had to be turned in before the end of the semester only required a final read-through.

What he did worry about was the lack of liquor in his house. Beer he had, enough to float himself across Lake Ontario. But he wanted something stronger. Sweatpants, an old flannel shirt, and a different pair of Converse—at least he wouldn't miss the ones he'd left at Jack's—took care of propriety.

Shuffling like an old man, he went down and out the kitchen door, heading for his mom's place.

He couldn't recall if she'd said she was going to be out or not, and wasn't sure if he hoped she was or wasn't, but she was out more often than not these days.

Turned out she wasn't home. Probably better if she didn't know right away he was going to swipe her booze.

A few minutes later, he stood in front of his mom's alarmingly sparse liquor cabinet, composed almost entirely of atrocities like flavored cream liqueurs and raspberry zinfandel. His father would have been appalled. Devlin let out a watery chuckle. No, his father would have busted a gut laughing.

Nevertheless, Devlin could probably do some damage with the blueberry vodka. With his hand on the bottle, he paused. It hadn't been so long ago that he'd tried drowning his sorrows in alcohol, with more reliable spirits than blueberry vodka. The only good thing that had come out of that night had been Jack, who'd been so gentle and caring. Sweet, even. It certainly hadn't done anything to erase his emotions.

Getting drunk tonight would likely accomplish even less, except a much more unpleasant hangover, and no Jack to take care of him. He was all alone.

Devlin snatched his hand back. He might be lonely, but he wasn't alone. He had his mom, as well as Ken and the other guys at Excalibur. It might be slow going, but he'd proven he could make new friends, and if he found himself at loose ends, well, he'd already seen the pages and pages of club listings the university had sanctioned, as well as volunteering at any number of the charities that he supported financially.

Losing himself in a bottle would appall his father and disappoint his mother, and Trent would kick his ass, if he were here.

Besides, he had an early class in the morning—with a new professor, since he'd changed his mind about dropping out. Devlin curled up on the couch with his grandmother's quilt and started browsing movie selections. He really hoped Jack hadn't ruined Indiana Jones for him, but he wasn't about to test that theory out just yet. Instead he pulled up *Galaxy Quest* again, since he'd fallen asleep while watching last time he'd sacked out in his mom's place trying to not feel alone.

ABOUT HALFWAY through the movie, his mom came home.

"Oh, hey, kid. Wasn't expecting to see you here tonight." No, probably not. When he hadn't been socializing, he'd been studying in his own house and falling asleep in his own bed, dreaming of filthy delicious things he could do to Jack or Jack could do to him.

"Yeah, me neither." He was supposed to fall asleep next to his freshly fucked brand-new boyfriend and commute to the university together, wearing the same clothes he'd worn the day before, like a rite of fucking passage.

He sniffed, and his mom tossed her purse on the hall table and came right to the couch, staring him in the face.

"Oh, baby." She sank down beside him, and Devlin leaned into her. Maybe a man his age shouldn't find comfort with his mother, but he appreciated the fact he could, unlike poor Jack.

She grabbed the remote and turned down the movie but let it continue to play as they sat there together.

After several minutes, she finally spoke. "Want to talk about it?"

Funny thing was, unlike Trent, he did want to talk about it. "Maybe."

Then he paused the movie and started to speak, tell her all the things about Jack she hadn't known from their one encounter in the kitchen.

He was pretty sure he'd managed to hide the few fresh tears he'd shed at the retelling.

She hugged him close. "Well, kid, what do *you* think?"

"I don't *know*. I don't know anything about having a boyfriend. Clearly. But how could I have missed that Jack was lying to me? How could I ever trust him again?"

That last question was telling. Somewhere in his mind, he'd thought about getting back together; he'd considered a way to make it work despite it all.

His mom sighed. "I'm just going to throw this out there. You've been pretty adamant about cutting the band out of your life. Angry when someone brings it up. I think… well, it's your decision, but you are well aware I'd like you to reconsider that decision. You cut me slack because I'm your mom and you're used to me nagging you. I think it's entirely possible Jack really didn't know how or when to tell you that he listened to Negative Impression. That he was part of a tribute band."

The glee in her voice was enough to tell him that if things were different between him and Jack, she'd insist on attending one of Crimson Corrosion's shows. His parents had been to a number of his own shows, so she well knew what she'd be getting into.

"But I also understand your hesitation. Thing is, I think I'm a pretty good judge of character. And I think you are too. Get it from me, no doubt."

Devlin grinned, the way he was supposed to. "And your point?"

"My point is that you've never once fallen for any of those overzealous fans with hidden agendas."

"True." Luke not only attracted more crazy than the rest of them put together, but he never once twigged to the crazy until it was restraining order time. Devlin had filed a few restraining orders, but never for guys he'd slept with.

"You think I overreacted." Just like Jack did.

She shrugged. "I wasn't there. But since that was your first guess, I think maybe you did overreact, and you know it. Sometimes we adults have to talk things out, you know."

Devlin snorted. "I'm forty-one years old. I've been adulting a long time."

"But never with a boyfriend."

"I'll think about it, okay?" And he would. He'd probably think it to death. Didn't mean he'd do anything about it. Because he wasn't sure he could trust Jack, no matter what they talked about.

His mom turned the movie back on, and they watched to the end in comforting silence.

CHAPTER TWELVE

DEVLIN STARED at the practical exercise and sighed. The last archaeology lab before exams and the winter break. Almost three weeks since he'd stormed out of Jack's apartment.

Trent's death had been devastating, and Devlin still missed him like an amputated limb, but he hadn't realized that since Jack walked into his life, he'd started remembering what happy had been like. The past three weeks without even a sighting of Jack had shown him the difference, and it sucked more than he'd ever have expected.

Professor Redmond gave archaeology a completely different vibe—or maybe that had to do with his complete lack of attraction to her, however cute she was. His classes were going well. But he missed Jack more than he'd ever have thought. He'd even started keeping track of Crimson Corrosion shows—not that he'd ever go. They had a show every Saturday in December until the week before Christmas.

For some, that might be a surprise, but back when he'd done his own booking for the band, December had been busy for Negative Impression too. He'd never looked into it, but he thought maybe people needed something to counteract the sugary sweetness of the Christmas season. Or maybe there were fewer non-Christmas things to do as alternatives in December. Last Saturday he'd even driven past the venue—four or five times—but never got a glimpse of Jack.

Staying away from Jack's office hours had been harder than he'd thought. He hadn't realized how much he'd come to rely on Jack's presence, Jack's input, Jack's conversation… and that was over and above Jack's kisses and the way he came apart in bed.

He heaved out another sigh.

"You okay?" Debbie, his regular lab partner, placed a gentle hand on his forearm.

"Yeah, just… man troubles."

A tiny laugh sputtered out of her, and Devlin frowned.

"Sorry, sorry, I didn't mean to laugh, but I just said that same thing to a friend not two hours ago. It sucks, doesn't it?"

"Yeah. I wish I could say being older makes it better, but it doesn't."

"Bleak."

Devlin shrugged.

"Me and my friends are hitting a club tomorrow. Drinks and dancing, keep our mind off men who make us miserable. Want to come along?"

It wasn't the first time she'd invited him—in fact, she was the reason he'd ended up at Ciao that first night, when he'd seen Jack with a date and confirmed for a fact the man was gay. Debbie and her friends were sweet, but he didn't think he had the balls to go into that club again, not when Jack's memory was so strong and the music was so not him. Or Jack either. He hadn't been lying about that.

Besides, he had a club to circle like a hungry shark on Saturday night. "Thanks, Debbie. I appreciate the offer, but I have plans."

"Just not with the man making you sigh."

He smiled sadly. "No, not really."

"If you change your mind, we'll be at Ciao, probably around ten."

They finished off the practical exercise, but all Dev could think about was his inability to shove all these feelings back under wraps where they couldn't cause him any trouble.

After the lab he went to the bathroom. He didn't really have to go, but it was almost a pilgrimage now. It was the same bathroom where he'd tried to help Jack through some sort of panic attack or food poisoning or whatever.

He'd also walk past Jack's office when he knew Jack was teaching other classes. He desperately missed their office hours, but those were reserved for Jack's students, not a stupid ex-boyfriend who couldn't let shit go, even though he'd been the one to break things off.

One day Jack was going to catch him at it, and that would be humiliating beyond words. Almost as humiliating as the fact that Dev hadn't deleted one of Jack's voicemails. He hadn't had the nerve to listen to them. He didn't know if Jack wanted him back, wanted to apologize, or merely called him every vicious name in existence. But he hadn't been able to hit that Delete icon. He certainly didn't have that same problem when Mo or Luke left him messages.

And he was starting to think that might be significant.

SATURDAY NIGHT, well after the start of the show, Devlin started circling the tiny club where Crimson Corrosion played. He'd thought about paying the car service to drive him around, but then he'd be tempted to drink too, and that sounded like a recipe for disaster. Bad enough that he was acting like a lovelorn teen; no one else needed to witness him doing it.

This was definitely the right place—lots of black leather and ass-kicking steel-toed boots went in. Less hair dyed black and more dyed every color of the rainbow, but Devlin liked the contradiction to the unrelieved monotone.

On his fourth pass around the club, a curbside spot two doors down from the club was open, and before he thought about it too hard, he pulled in.

It felt a bit like the universe was trying to tell him something.

Did he dare do this? He sat there for long minutes as he considered all angles. It all boiled down to three key elements. One: he probably had let his temper get the better of him at Jack's apartment. Two: it was likely that Jack was guilty of nothing more than poor judgment and nothing nefarious. Three, and this was the one that held more weight than anything else: Dev missed Jack so fucking much. More than he'd ever have expected, and when they'd gotten together, he'd already started imagining a future that held Jack in it. Stupidly or not, he still wanted that.

Was it possible to work things out? Or had Devlin waited too long?

He ran through all the possibilities, but no matter what scenario he imagined, nothing kept him from wanting to walk through the door of that club, even if it meant facing his music. Somehow missing Jack had eclipsed his knee-jerk avoidance of anything related to Negative Impression.

A glance at the time told him he'd been sitting here far too long, and he ran the risk of missing Jack if he waited too much longer.

AS WAS his longtime habit, Devlin ditched his jacket in the car and sprinted through the cold December night to the front door. Checking a jacket was a fucking pain in the ass, and it wasn't like he could leave the jacket with friends. Hell, he'd lost a jacket at Ciao the night Jack had taken him home because he'd been too drunk to remember he'd been wearing one when he went to the club.

In the shadows near the door, Devlin hung back. Smoking indoors had been banned for a long time, and yet the pall of long-dead cigarettes hung in the air, along with the stale scent of spilled beer and clashing body odor. Just like every tiny venue Negative Impression had played back in the day. And for the next twenty years too. The venues got bigger, but the smells never really changed.

The chords of "Of This Corrosion" were easily recognizable. His shoulders tensed, and a muscle jumped in his jaw as he waited for the pain. And it was there, to be sure, but like Jack had tried to tell him, there were memories—good ones—that this song invoked: the time in London when someone threw a teddy bear at Trent; the practice in Brussels where Luke's keyboard had shorted out and caught fire, funny afterward, when they confirmed no one had been hurt; and the celebration when they found out the single had gone platinum, when they'd never had any expectation of real commercial success.

Good times. Good memories. And Crimson Corrosion, while they played with the tune a little, altering it slightly from the original, did a good job of it. Jack sounded good. They didn't sound the same, and maybe that made it easier. Or maybe it didn't matter as much as he'd thought.

They finished "Of This Corrosion" and led right into "Crimson in the Vein." So many memories in this song. They'd started the lyrics in high school, years before they met Luke and Mo. But they'd forgotten about it until Trent moved to a new apartment and the band helped him. A whole notebook of scribblings, chords, choruses, snippets of lyrics practically fell at their feet, inspiring a week of intensive brainstorming, which culminated in their best-selling album.

Dev suspected this was the last song. It made sense to end with Negative Impression's most popular song. Dev made his way through the darkened club to get closer to the stage. A small throng of dancers bounced in front of the band, which he'd only really glimpsed through peripheral vision, a little afraid to look at Jack.

"Of This Corrosion." "Crimson in the Vein." Jack's band name had combined the titles of their most popular songs, and Dev hadn't even realized. Clever. And not painful. He should have let Jack tell him about this, because he was good. The whole band was good. And for a long time, playing music had been the best job Dev had ever had. He should have shared this with Jack.

At the edge of the dance floor, he came to a stop, inhaled deeply, then brought his gaze to the stage.

With only his profile visible, the air of melancholy around Jack struck him first. It imbued "Crimson in the Vein" with an entirely different feel, amping up the desolation, and Dev couldn't help but feel responsible. He wore tight black jeans and a black T-shirt, hugging all of Jack's assets.

Then Jack turned, facing the audience head-on. Product had his hair spiking up all over, rather than exactly mimicking the Mohawk Dev had let grow in just this year. Thick black eyeliner ringed those pale blue eyes. He hadn't gone for the full-on crimson lips but wore a shade of burgundy so dark it was almost as black as the eyeliner. He looked so fucking perfect, just as Dev had imagined.

But not only did he look perfect, he looked familiar. This man was.... Dev gripped his hands into fists as he stared. Time didn't change his impression. He knew this man, but not as Dr. Jack, his sexy archaeology professor.

His breathing sped up. This was another lie. Another fucking lie, and he nearly ran up to the stage. Wanted to jump up there with Jack and confront him.

But… he'd come here for answers, and maybe this was yet another answer he needed. Maybe they couldn't fix things between them, but Devlin was working without all the facts.

"Crimson in the Vein" drew to a close, and Dev slipped away before the house lights came up. He needed answers, but this wasn't the time or place. Except, now that he was ready, he didn't want to wait.

Back in his car, the temperature had already cooled down to icy. Clearly the reason for his trembling. No other explanation was possible.

He sat there for a few minutes, tapping the steering wheel with his fingers. The coffee shop Jack took him to on Trent's birthday wasn't far. He could text Jack, ask him to meet there. There were no guarantees, but he needed to see Jack, and he didn't much want an audience for it.

He grimaced. There was only one thing that fit the bill, but it was something he'd never, ever thought he'd do to someone. Desperate times and all that.

JACK PARKED his car behind his apartment building and got out. Icy wind, an omen of winter to come, sliced through him, and he shivered. His building was older, and didn't have underground parking, only a covered lot for residents, uncovered for visitors. Days, and nights—like tonight—it sucked, but he did like his apartment and its convenience to the subway and its much lower rent than somewhere closer to the university.

He was fucking exhausted, and not for the first time in recent weeks had he thought about quitting Crimson Corrosion. How much of his emotional well-being could he wrap up in one band? All of it, apparently.

"Jack?"

And now he was hallucinating. He ignored the voice that sounded altogether too much like Devlin's and got out his keys.

"Please. Jack. We have to talk."

Jack's breath hitched. Devlin was here. Apparently waiting in his parking lot for him to come home. Would he still be here if Jack had agreed to go out for drinks with the band afterward? Or if he'd taken up that cute young guy in the audience on his blatant invitation?

Edged on stalkerish behavior, and yet, when he turned, the sight of Devlin was so welcome, like the sight of water after getting lost in the desert, that he couldn't be upset.

Then again, Devlin had ignored his voicemails for nearly three weeks. Left Jack to scour news sites, making sure nothing had happened to Devlin when he drove off, so angry and upset.

Devlin looked jaundiced and ill, but the yellowish lights illuminating the parking lot weren't flattering to anyone. Unflattering light or not, Devlin appeared a bit thinner, and there was no hiding the smudges under his eyes. Smudges that matched Jack's when he removed the eyeliner.

Jack breathed slowly. Devlin didn't look angry, but then, he didn't know what Jack had been up to.

"It's late." Like that mattered. Jack hadn't had a restful night's sleep since Devlin left.

"I know. I'm sorry, but I couldn't wait any longer."

For a man who kept all his emotions tied in a straightjacket, confined to a safe, further wrapped in chains, then tossed to the bottom of a lake, he had a problem with impulse control.

But if they were able to clear the air between them, get some closure, Jack might be able to move on. He'd hoped for weeks Devlin would relent and try to work this out, but fuck and run was his natural state, not being a boyfriend. He couldn't afford to hope for a reconciliation, not anymore. It was too damned painful.

"Fine." They were both shivering. Jack peered closely at Devlin but didn't see any indications that he wanted to, oh, cut him up into pieces. Aside from metaphorically. "Did you want to come up?"

Devlin nodded. Resigned to another long, sleepless night, accompanied by more tears after Devlin left again, Jack unlocked the door and let Devlin in.

The ride up in the elevator in its harsh fluorescent light, was awkward as fuck, and Jack hoped he didn't look as washed-out as he felt.

They stood beside each other, locked in stasis, neither of them wanting to start this discussion until they were behind closed doors.

Inside Jack's apartment, he still wasn't ready. "Did you want some coffee?"

"Yes, please, if it's not too much trouble."

"No trouble." Anything to postpone this.

Jack didn't turn on the overhead lights in the kitchen, just the softer one over the stove. It gave him plenty of light to make coffee and see each other by, but didn't feel like they were participating in a police interrogation.

Devlin sat at the table while Jack prepared a pot of coffee. "Caffeinated okay?" He had decaf, but he'd already ruled out sleeping tonight so he might as well drink the good stuff.

"That's fine. I like your kitchen. Feels warm, like my mom's."

"Thanks." The only time Devlin had been at his apartment, the tour had been cursory, since they'd both been more interested in the bedroom. Devlin probably hadn't even set foot in the kitchen last time.

Making coffee only put off the inevitable so long, and Jack set steaming mugs on the table before sitting down himself.

He opened his mouth to apologize, again, but Devlin beat him to the punch.

"Why did you tell me your name was Ryan?"

For long seconds Jack could only stare. "I don't even know how to answer that."

Devlin's lips flattened. "Shouldn't be that difficult. I thought about it all the way here, and I think I know why you didn't mention that we'd… uh… met before, but I can't figure out why you lied about your name."

Met before. That was a nice euphemism. Anger started bubbling up, a slow burn that had been building for four years. "You think you know why? How's this for starters? I *didn't* lie about my name. You're the one who called me Ryan out of the blue. I told you my name was Jack in the limo."

But honestly it hadn't been the name thing. There were men Jack had fucked who he'd never even asked for a name, nor had they asked for his. It was the name thing on top of the money thing on top of the shitty dismissive attitude that made it awful.

Devlin's mouth dropped open. "You… you're not joking, are you?"

"No, I'm not. For a long time, that was simultaneously the best and worst sexual experience of my life. Surpassed in both by our first time here in my apartment."

Oh fuck. Jack definitely was tired if he'd put that out there, seething in resentment and hurt.

"Jack…. JJ… I'm so sorry."

If the use of a nickname, one that Devlin had given him while drunk and stupid, was supposed to soften him up, well it was working, damn him. Helped that an apology came with it.

Devlin wrapped his hands around his mug. "God. I used to look for you. Any show we did in the Toronto area, even in Buffalo and Niagara Falls, I'd look for you, hoping you'd be there in the audience."

"Why?" Jack couldn't avoid the venom in his voice. He'd decided that he'd been holding on to his ire for no good reason, but talking about it now told him he hadn't let it go as successfully as he'd believed.

"I treated you so badly there at the end. You didn't deserve it, and you intrigued me."

"I intrigued you," Jack said flatly. "But you couldn't remember my name."

Devlin's gaze dropped to the table. "So, that was the first show we played after my dad died. I had… a hard time dealing with the rush of performing, the need to pretend everything was normal, when I was hurting inside. I drank too much, and I treated you like shit. I won't lie, I've fucked a lot of guys over the years, and there haven't always been names exchanged. Even so, I've done my best not to be an asshole. But I remembered you—how could I forget you? You were… gorgeous, in bed and out, and it wasn't just because I was a shit that made you memorable. I think… well, we both know that I don't do well when I'm trying to drink my feelings away."

Jack sat very still as his perceptions shifted. With those few words, Devlin was able to do what four years of self-castigation had not, and all the pain washed out of that memory. "No, you don't. You should maybe think about not doing that."

Devlin quirked a sad smile. "Already realized that. I didn't drown my sorrows in my mother's blueberry vodka the night I left here."

Jack couldn't help but grimace. "Blueberry vodka?"

"It was tempting. For a few seconds, anyway."

"Good. I'm glad." He sighed. "What the hell triggered that memory anyway? I recognized your name right off. I mean, I thought it was simply a coincidence, because I've never seen you without makeup and without the black Mohawk. But that first lab, when you started flirting so hard, you lifted up your shirt, and I saw your tattoo. The band logo. That's when I knew it was really you, and I freaked out. Because I have been carrying around some baggage from that encounter."

Devlin let go of his mug, and his hands hovered for a moment before he reached over and gripped Jack's hands tightly. "Seriously, I'm so sorry. Once I realized you were Ryan, and well, I've had a couple hours in your parking lot to think about things. I think that night four years ago probably affected a lot of your decisions. Because you had chances to tell me you knew about the band, and you had chances to tell me about Crimson Corrosion, and you didn't. I can only assume that was because you were trying to avoid confronting me about that night."

Jack huffed in surprise. When Devlin tried, he did pretty well with this emotional stuff.

"Pretty much, yeah. I… resented you, and disliked you, but I was also your professor, and I was desperately trying to be both impartial and professional. Obviously that didn't work out as well as I'd hoped."

A flash of sadness crossed Devlin's face. "You started liking me. For a while at least."

Killing him. Devlin was going to twist him up in knots before he was done. "I still like you." The words almost choked him on the way out, because it was nothing more than the pathetic, bitter truth. Partial truth. Even after all the pain he'd endured, he more than liked

Devlin, a feeling that had gotten so much stronger over the several weeks they'd gotten to know each other.

Devlin nodded but didn't return the sentiment, damn him. "As for the trigger, I, uh, was at your show tonight."

Oh God. There had been a part of him that had been glad Devlin eschewed all Negative Impression things. If he'd known he'd been singing Blade's songs for Blade himself, he'd have probably wet himself right there on stage. But that explained how Devlin had recognized him. When he'd gone to that fateful Negative Impression show, he'd dressed exactly the same way he did when he was singing for Crimson Corrosion.

"You came to the show?" More importantly… "You came to the show and listened while we were playing Negative Impression songs?"

"I did."

Jack peered intently in Devlin's eyes. "Was it hard? I mean…." Jack bit his lip. "Was it too painful?" They both knew Jack wasn't asking for a compliment.

Devlin's smile was real, if not terribly wide. "It was… good. You were right about the memories. There are far more good ones than bad."

Jack's eyes started burning, but he swallowed heavily trying to chase away the tears, no matter how happy they were.

"You were right about a lot of things, and I've been a jerk. An asshole. And I'm so sorry. I know I keep saying that, but I don't know how else to tell you. I've dealt with things poorly, and I intend to get better. But Jack, I've missed you so much. Do you think you could give me another chance? I don't really know how to be a boyfriend, but I hope I didn't fuck up too badly."

Jack couldn't breathe. Couldn't believe he was hearing these words. "You fucked up bad. I haven't been sleeping. I keep trying to find excuses to walk past the Intro archaeology class, and forcing myself not to. Your complete radio silence hurt me."

"Please. Is there any way I can make it up to you?"

Was he really going to do this? Was he really going to give Devlin the chance to destroy him again? But if Devlin really was on board, didn't he have a chance for a happy-ever-after like other people got?

"You can't ever walk out on me like that again, no matter what. I was afraid you were so upset you'd gotten into a car accident. Then you wouldn't return my phone calls. I was worried sick and furious and hurt all at the same time. I know you said you don't know how to be a boyfriend. Well, it's important to talk out things like this, not just storm off."

"I promise." Devlin's voice was shaky but sincere. "I promise. Because I hated it too, and… it was my emotional issues that caused all of our problems. I missed you, JJ."

Jack shifted his hands so they were both holding on. There would be time to talk about Devlin's avoidance of Luke and Mo, but tonight, Jack was only interested in repairing his own relationship. "I missed you too."

"So… are we back together?" Devlin was so unsure, but strangely, Jack wasn't.

"We are. Ever hear of something called makeup sex?"

This time, Devlin's smile was wide and happy. "Never tried it, but I'm feeling inspired."

Jack laughed, and if there was a hysterical edge to it, Devlin was kind enough not to comment.

Devlin drew him to his feet and kissed him gently, and the memory of Devlin, aka Blade, in bed suddenly morphed to excellent sexual experiences, ones he was eager to replicate. With his boyfriend.

CHAPTER THIRTEEN

IT WAS too much to expect the rest of their relationship to continue in such an idyllic manner forevermore, but Devlin had been happier in the past week, since he and Jack had gotten together, than he'd been in a long time.

Their schedules were messed up, since there were no scheduled classes until January, and they both had exams: Devlin had to take them, Jack had to proctor and mark them. But around that? They'd had lunch around campus when it didn't interfere with exams. Splitting time between both of their places, they'd spent a lot of time talking, watching television, and fucking. Devlin had taken Jack to his mom's and introduced Jack to her properly as his boyfriend.

She'd been thrilled, and Jack had been tearily overwhelmed. Devlin might need a lot of guidance to become a decent boyfriend, but he had an awesome mom, and hopefully she might make up for any of his deficiencies.

Devlin was lucky. As of today all of his exams were done. Some poor bastards had exams right up until the Friday before Christmas. Jack had a few exams to proctor the following week, but Devlin was hoping he could take them both home today, spend the whole weekend together, then convince Jack to stay with him until at least the start of classes in January.

Sort of test case of moving in together. Fast, to be sure, but Devlin had been around long enough to know what he wanted, and he wanted Jack in his place. Jack's apartment was closer to the university in pure distance, but from Devlin's place, they could easily take the GO Train instead of the subway, or Devlin always had a car service he could call.

Devlin stepped outside and breathed in the sharp, cold air of mid-December. The sky was overcast, and fat, fluffy flakes drifted from the sky. Done. His first set of exams was done, and he nailed them. It was a long way from a successful first semester to a degree, and then possibly a graduate degree, but this convinced him he wasn't fooling himself. Now he had proof he could do it. He was ready and eager for the next chapter in his life, one that had Jack at his side.

There was a little bounce in his step as he made his way to the building with Jack's office. Once inside, he walked the now-familiar and almost comforting route to Jack's office. Jack's dark head bent studiously over his desk made Devlin smile. Taking joy in the everyday things—part of what having a boyfriend, someone he maybe loved, was all about, as Devlin was discovering.

He knocked on the doorframe, and Jack looked up, startled.

"Oh, hi. Done already?"

"Yes. Nailed it."

Jack smiled. "Good. I knew you would."

"Ready to go?"

"Yeah, I can take off early today."

"Good." Devlin smiled. "Want me to call the car service? We could stop at your place for some clothes and things.... I was thinking you could spend the weekend at my place, no studying, no marking, just... a wee vacation."

They could go shopping if Jack was into that. For a badass punk rocker, Devlin actually liked the bustle and cheer of shopping malls at Christmastime, but that attitude wasn't common, or so he understood.

Or they could figure out what Devlin needed to make his mausoleum of a house into a home. Jack obviously had the knack, since his apartment was cozy as all get-out. Devlin wanted Jack's input, since he really was hoping Jack would give up his apartment eventually and move in. The house needed to be a blend of them both.

Jack wasn't exactly jumping for joy at this idea, though, judging by the grimace twisting his lips.

Devlin shrugged. "It's fine. We don't have to. It was just a thought."

Jack rounded his desk and peeked out in the hall before giving him a quick kiss. "It's a great idea. Really. I mean, I want to spend time with you, and maybe we can use that awesome fireplace you've got."

Oh yeah. Some thick fuzzy blankets on the floor, a roaring fire, and a naked boyfriend. Maybe with beer and pizza… that would be just perfect.

"Sounds great. So why the hesitation?" Look at Devlin asking questions calmly. He was getting the hang of this boyfriend thing.

Jack winced. "It's just… I've got a show. Crimson Corrosion. Last show of the year on Saturday."

Right. He knew that. Just, he wasn't sure how he felt, confronted with it again.

"I… did you want me to quit? I mean, I have to do this show on Saturday, but maybe they can find someone else to sing." Jack shrugged. "It's not like I play an instrument."

Devlin did his best to wade past his knee-jerk avoidance response that he'd trained for the past several months. He remembered Jack's image onstage, which was sexy as hell. Some of the things they'd discussed since getting back together had been Jack's love of Negative Impression and how it had helped him through his teen years when his dad's verbal abuse intensified because he wanted Jack to be more "manly."

No denying it was a little odd that when he'd been little more than a teen himself, he'd been a role model of sorts for a man he was now dating, but it made him realize that Negative Impression wasn't some ego-boosting tool just for him. The music was out there, the feelings and sentiments in the lyrics were out there, and as soon as they hit the airwaves, they weren't really for him anymore. At least, not entirely.

His earlier refusal to even talk about Negative Impression didn't change that fact; it only made him seem selfish.

"You are great up there. It's harder to find a good singer than you think, even for a punk band that occasionally uses voice modulation. And… I can tell from the way you talk about it, you have fun doing it. At least when I haven't been a dick and wrecked it for you."

Jack smiled sadly. "I can't tell if that's a yes or not."

Devlin breathed deeply and steeled himself. "No. Please don't quit on my account. I… I can't guarantee I'll be able to come see you. Not yet. But you can still come and spend the weekend." He shrugged. "I can entertain myself Saturday night."

"You realize if I stick with it, there will be rehearsals and stuff too, right?"

Devlin tilted his head to the side. "You mean… musicians have to practice? That's just crazy enough to work!" He might not have been quite as lighthearted as his joke made him sound, but it was worth it to see the worry ease from Jack's face. "I may not have had a boyfriend before, but I do know we don't have to be in each other's pockets all the time. We're allowed to have our own lives and interests."

Jack pressed up close, although not quite to the point of impropriety—one day he would let Devlin blow him under his desk, but today was not that day. "They want to meet up for a late dinner first, then head over to the club. But I'll rush right home after."

"I'll be fine. We'll be fine." Especially since Jack had inadvertently called Devlin's house home.

Jack moved away and stuffed papers and exams into his bag before pulling on his jacket. "You know you're always welcome. Socializing with my friends, showing up at a gig. Whenever you're ready, you can come along any time. The invitation is always open."

"Thank you." Devlin appreciated there was no ultimatum, no deadline, and one day he'd take Jack up on it. Not just for Jack, but for himself and Trent too.

"JESUS YOU look hot like this."

Jack's hair was spiked up. He had on those sinfully tight black jeans, and tight black T-shirt. Devlin usually wore black leather and Doc Martens to his shows, but Jack wore Converse. The only thing missing was the eyeliner and lip color. As soon as that was applied, Jack would be off to his Saturday-night show, while Devlin prepared for delivered dinner and a quiet night of relaxation.

Jack's cheeks pinked right up. "Stop."

Devlin wiggled his eyebrows. "You make sure you tell 'em your boyfriend is jealous."

There wasn't much better in this world than making Jack laugh, except maybe when he made him come.

"How come you never wear leather pants?"

Jack shuddered. "Seriously, I don't know how you don't pass out from the heat in those things."

Devlin shrugged. "No job is perfect."

That got him an eye roll. "First year I did this, I saved up and bought a pair, because, newsflash, those things aren't cheap. Every show I bathed in sweat, and I thought my balls were going to broil. Then, after about six months, I ripped the shit out of those pants. Accidental, and I didn't have the money for new ones, so I wore black jeans, fully intending to purchase another pair. But it was so damn nice and cool wearing jeans, I couldn't ever bring myself to spend that much money to torture myself."

"So I guess you don't want to wear one of my old pairs, eh? We're probably close enough in size that you'd be okay."

For a second, Jack looked thoughtful, and almost covetous, amusing the fuck out of Devlin.

"No, I don't think so. I prefer the jeans."

"What about one of my vests? You could just pop it over your shirt."

Jack almost bounced on his feet. "Yeah, that'd be cool. I must admit, I'm sort of surprised you kept all that stuff."

Devlin was too, in a way. He hadn't changed his everyday look, but his "show" clothes were different: more expensive, more elaborate, and just… more. By rights, he should have ditched it all when he'd decided to end Negative Impression. But he'd held on to it, stored in one of the guest rooms just like always. Perhaps that should have told him he hadn't entirely closed the door on all things musical.

"Let's see how it looks." Jack followed him into the guest room, and just the smell of all that leather evoked more memories. More good memories. He wasn't about to start reminiscing about every damned piece, though, and headed straight for his vests. He pulled out a simple one, just a few zippers on it. Jack held it gingerly, reverently, before he slipped it on.

"Yeah. Leather looks good on you, JJ." Only a hint of melancholy came through in his words, Devlin was proud to note.

"Thanks. I'll take good care of it. No rips in this, I promise."

"If it rips, it rips. It's a vest, not the Magna Carta."

Jack let out a sputter of surprised laughter.

"You gonna put on your makeup here?"

"No. I'll wait until right before I go on stage."

Devlin followed Jack downstairs. "Have fun. You've got the number for the car service, right?"

"Yes, I promise. But Stephanie probably won't want to stay late, and she'll drop me off."

"Just in case. It's always an option." Oakville from downtown could be a pain in the wee hours of the morning, and whatever Jack said about leaving right after the show, Devlin knew how easy it was to get sidetracked. He wasn't expecting him back until 2:00 a.m. at least.

Devlin kissed Jack, and Jack moaned into it and pulled away. "Stop that. I don't want to get on stage all horny and hours to go before you fuck me."

Smiling wide, Devlin watched him walk down the drive and through the gate to wait for Stephanie. That had been Jack's decision, because he'd worried that Stephanie might overwhelm him or might push too hard on Devlin's memories. But there was a plan in place to meet up with Stephanie and her husband for brunch soon, at a neutral location to make it easier for Devlin.

He thought it sweet Jack was trying to protect him, but he had to admit it unsettled him a bit. Mostly because Jack shouldn't have to protect him from his friends. Something didn't sit quite right about that.

AN HOUR later, the silence in his house almost oppressive, Devlin finished his Chinese food and lounged in bed, flicking through movie options. Nothing grabbed his attention, but there were hundreds or thousands more options. Eventually he'd find something.

"Hey, kid, where are you?"

Dev sat up in bed, panic freezing him for a second before he launched himself to his feet and dragged on sweatpants. Devlin dropped by his mother's place unannounced all the time, but she never dropped by his place like that.

He dashed down the stairs. Something must be wrong, and his heart pounded in fear.

"What's wrong?" He rocked to a stop by the kitchen door, phone in hand, ready to call 911.

"Nothing's wrong, except you're not dressed."

Devlin looked down at himself, then at her. "I'm dressed, but I don't know why you're dressed like that."

His mom was dressed like… well, like she used to dress back when Negative Impression started getting gigs. She and his father had both gone to early shows. It had been a bit embarrassing that his parents were so supportive that they'd show up, but the rest of the band thought it was cute… and a way to mock Devlin mercilessly when his parents weren't around. Win-win for them. But as their popularity grew and the venues got more and more packed, his parents stopped coming. Been close to fifteen years since his mom had gone to one of his shows.

"Jack's playing tonight, right? I thought we could go down together."

Holy shit. He'd thought nothing of it when Jack had gone over to his mom's place without him that morning for breakfast, because Devlin really did have a hard time waking up. Jack must have told her about the show.

"Did he ask you to come? Did he tell you I was going?"

His mother frowned. "Not in so many words. He just mentioned it more or less in passing. I *assumed* you'd be going to be supportive, and I thought I'd tag along."

Devlin just stared at her. He wanted to say he wasn't ready. He wanted to say he'd been plenty supportive. But maybe he hadn't. And he was well aware his mother wasn't as guileless as she appeared. She thought this would be good for him.

Maybe she was right. Devlin also wanted to meet Jack's friends. If they were going to truly mesh their lives, then that had to be part of it.

"Promise I can leave if it's too much." One show. If he freaked out, then he could leave and try again in the New Year, at another of Jack's shows.

Her eyes softened. "Of course, kid. But you're stronger than you think."

The decision solved all the things that had unsettled him about letting Jack go off on his own, which confirmed it had to be the right course of action.

"I'll go get changed."

"Hurry up, I don't want to be late."

JACK SURVEYED the crowd, smaller than the past few shows, but then again, it was damned close to Christmas. For the first time since he'd gotten to know Devlin, he was not divided about singing Negative Impression songs. There was no twinge of resentment, no need to avoid thinking of Devlin, no worry that he was somehow deceiving Devlin. Wearing Devlin's leather vest gave him a little extra boost, like a badge of honor.

The music was almost as simple and uncomplicated as it had been before he'd slept with Blade four years ago. The only change was he now had a bunch of secondhand stories about a man who had been tremendously important to his boyfriend, and it saddened Jack he'd never gotten a chance to know Trent.

His soul was lighter, but melancholy threaded through each tune. The rest of the band went with it, and when they deviated from the songs as they were written, they'd added haunting hints of melodies in minor keys.

Maybe Devlin wouldn't approve of the modifications, but Devlin wasn't here. One day, though, Devlin would be here, making Jack nervous. He'd all but promised, and Jack was going to hold him to it, when he was ready. It hadn't been a year yet, since Trent died; plenty of time to come for Devlin to face his ghosts.

He came to the end of "Moon Dark" and wiped sweat out of his eyes. Jeans might be cooler than leather pants, but stage lights were still hot as Hades.

"Thanks, guys. We'll be back on in thirty."

The rest of the band stowed their equipment to take a break, and they sat at the table that had been reserved for them. Sometimes they took their break in the back, away from the crowds, but today had a mellow vibe, and they chanced it. Sitting in the bar was more comfortable, as long as they weren't mobbed.

A few fans came up and talked to them, including one guy who came to a number of shows and clearly wanted Jack to take him home.

This time the guy sat down next to him, rubbing up against him like a cat while he cooed about Jack's singing. Jack kept shuffling his chair away, but pretty soon there would be nowhere to go, and then he'd have to spell things out. Beyond the "I'm sorry, I'm seeing someone" he'd already told him.

"Oh, honey, you should move along now. You did know our Jack was taken, didn't you?"

They both swung their heads around to face the speaker. Jack completely lost his words at seeing Beth, dressed in black and blending into the crowd surprisingly well considering she seemed a "sweater set and pearls" sort of woman.

"By you?" The boy's incredulity was… perhaps warranted since Jack made no secret of his orientation. But it was also a little insulting, and that let him find his words.

"No need to be rude. This is my boyfriend's mother."

The kid flushed, mumbled something, then slunk away.

Beth smiled at him. "You did a great job, Jack, dear." She leaned over and kissed his cheek before sitting down in an empty chair. "I'm sorry we were late, but we saw most of the set."

Jack's stomach fluttered, and his mouth dried out. "We?" he squeaked, then sucked back a mouthful of vodka and cranberry. "Devlin's here?" That had to be "we," didn't it?

"Of course he is, dear. He just had to show up and support you."

Jack stared at the woman who he hoped would one day be his mother-in-law. He had a feeling she'd ruthlessly taken advantage of the crack in the dam that Jack had so carefully cultivated and forced her way through. Showing up to support him had to have been her idea, but she'd brought Devlin, and that meant everything.

"Where is he?"

"Getting fresh drinks. He'll be along in a moment. Introduce me to your friends."

"Oh, of course."

Everyone was well aware of the identity of Jack's boyfriend, and they were almost giddy as they greeted Devlin's mother, anticipating Devlin's arrival at the table like kids in line for Santa Claus.

Devlin arrived at the table with a beer and a glass of wine—he hadn't even known the bar stocked wine—and sat between Jack and his mother.

"Hello, everyone. I'm Devlin. Jack's boyfriend." The words alone were capable of giving Jack a thrill, but the warmth and pride in Devlin's voice made his heart beat faster.

Jack introduced Devlin to his friends, and even Stephanie behaved with decorum. Devlin was gracious in the face of their intense regard, but then, he'd had twenty years of practice.

Devlin complimented all of the band members on their performance, but after they offered their condolences, he let his mother carry most of the conversation. This had to be so hard for Devlin, but it was an amazing step toward healing.

Jack squeezed his knee and leaned into his ear to whisper, "I'm so proud of you, and I'm so happy you're here."

Devlin turned and kissed him, quick and hard. "You kill it in the next set. Then we're going home and settling in."

Home. Yes, he'd definitely started thinking of Devlin's place as home, and he had a feeling Devlin didn't mind that one bit.

"Right. I guess it's about that time," Barry said as he stood. "Devlin, Beth, it's been a real pleasure meeting you, and I hope we'll see you around often."

Kirk and Ann shook Devlin's hand again and hugged Beth. Stephanie hugged both of them, which Devlin endured stoically. Jack kissed him on the temple, then followed the band to the stage.

AS USUAL they'd saved "Of This Corrosion" and "Crimson in the Vein" for the end. While Barry and Ann played the final chords for "Of This Corrosion," Devlin hopped up on the stage, a determined look on his face.

Could he… could Devlin want to sing "Crimson in the Vein"? Jack offered the mic, but Devlin shook his head and stepped up to Barry, miming something. Barry nodded enthusiastically and took off his guitar to hand it to Devlin.

When Devlin set the guitar across his body, Jack just about fainted dead away. Then Jack realized Devlin had requested to sub in for the wrong part. Ann was their bassist, and Devlin should have taken her instrument.

Then Devlin played the familiar intro to "Crimson in the Vein." The guitar intro that had been Trent's alone. Jack had no idea that Devlin could play Trent's parts, but the rest of the band picked up his lead. Barry shifted so he was sharing the mic with Jack, and they both sang.

Partway through the song, Jack glanced over and saw tears streaming unchecked down Devlin's face as he played Trent's guitar solo with skill and love. By some miracle Jack kept his own tears at bay, if only to avoid having his voice crack and ruin Devlin's tribute to the friend he loved and lost. A glance over at the band's table showed Beth, wiping her eyes with a tissue. Checking the rest of the band, it was clear they were also affected, but they continued playing, and played their best, supporting Devlin's impromptu memorial.

No one else in the audience seemed aware of the poignant moment happening on stage. Maybe if Devlin had his hair spiked and dyed, or if his tattoos were on display, and he wasn't wearing tight blue jeans and a long-sleeved waffle-knit shirt.

Then again Devlin wasn't on stage to perform. He wasn't there to put on a show. He was saying goodbye, but he was also saying he wasn't going to forget.

The last of the chords faded away, and Jack dropped the mic, leaping over to Devlin, shoving the guitar to the side, and wrapping him in a tight hug.

They shook and cried in each other's arms, heedless of the applause from the oblivious audience.

"Thank you," Devlin whispered brokenly into Jack's hair. "Thank you for giving me back the music."

EPILOGUE

"ISN'T IT time yet?" Jack asked.

Devlin laughed. He didn't think he'd ever seen anyone so excited about a Christmas dinner. It didn't even involve presents.

They'd exchanged presents early that morning before Devlin accompanied Jack to visit his father.

No wonder Jack found Devlin's mom so enthralling. From what Jack had told him, his father had been harsh, verbally abusive, and not particularly loving. Jack had long suspected his father blamed him for his mother leaving. But the way Alzheimer's had eaten his mind, to the point he was vicious in his epithets with everyone and had no recognition of Jack at all… well, he wouldn't wish that on his worst enemy. Or his worst enemy's family, since Jack bore the brunt of all those conflicted emotions.

Now that the obligatory visit was over, Jack was simply desperate for a Christmas with a loving family, and Devlin wanted this to be one of many he gave Jack over the years to come.

Jack had worked himself into knots, wondering what food they could contribute to dinner, but Devlin just laughed. His mom might like cooking, but part of Devlin's gift to her every year since the band had taken off was a catered Christmas dinner, with carte blanche for her to order whatever she wanted. Not exactly what people might expect from a badass punk rocker, but he wasn't exactly an active punk rocker anymore, and he no longer needed to maintain any sort of façade.

His mom probably had homemade cookies, but she much preferred watching sappy Christmas movies to slaving away in the kitchen. This year it wouldn't have been too bad, though, since it was only the three of them.

He gasped and wobbled. Jack spun on his heel, worry all over his face.

"What's wrong?"

Devlin breathed. "Just… realizing Trent won't be here for Christmas dinner. His parents died several years ago, so he spent every holiday with us. Luke and Mo would sometimes show up, sometimes my mom would invite everyone and their families over, but Trent was always there. And it's hard." Devlin's voice broke, but he continued. "It's hard, these milestones. All the firsts without him."

Jack hugged him. "I know it hurts. But just remember you're not alone."

Devlin's eyesight blurred as he hugged Jack back. "I know. And that means more than I can tell you."

They stood there, silently, until Devlin had composed himself again.

Jack finished getting ready—they'd gone back to bed and gotten dirty after opening presents—and finally Devlin said it was time.

Hand in hand, they walked the short distance to his mother's house. There was a low hum of sound coming from it, like she had the television or radio blasting. Weird, but perhaps he was simply hearing one of the neighbors having a particularly rowdy Christmas.

On the porch Jack pushed himself in front of Devlin and flung open the door. Christmas music and conversation—so much conversation—poured out into the cold, snowy day.

His mother's house was filled with people, like Christmases past, and Devlin froze.

"Come on. It's okay. They're all friends." Jack tugged him inside.

The conversation stuttered to a halt. Front and center stood Luke and Mo, anxiety clear in their expressions.

Fuck. He'd been an idiot. Trent had been like a brother to him, but so had Luke and Mo. They'd gone through so much together, and they'd lost Trent too. Devlin had been grieving in a solitary silo, and he'd not had to.

Devlin took a few faltering steps toward them. "I've missed you so much. I'm sorry."

Mo leaped at him and hugged him, Luke following a second later, a tremulous smile warming his face.

"It's good to see you," Mo said as the guy clench came to an end.

"Yes. And don't ever do that again."

Devlin nodded, and Jack appeared beside him. "Hello."

This time it was his turn to introduce Jack to his band, although he suspected Jack had had some involvement in this Christmas surprise.

Once that was done, Devlin allowed himself to pay attention to his mother's guests. Mo's and Luke's wives were there, and Mo's five-year-old daughter. Stephanie and her husband. Mo's dads, and Luke's parents. Full fucking house, and it was good.

DINNER HAD gone well. Several people told stories about Trent, and there were some tears, but Jack and his mother had been right. Sharing this with others who'd loved Trent helped more than it hurt. He really wasn't alone.

Mostly everyone had moved out of the dining room to watch *It's a Wonderful Life* or something his mom had put on, except for Jack, Mo, and Luke. Sitting with those three made Devlin content. Except for one thing, and maybe Christmas wasn't the best time to address it, but he'd been avoiding it for nearly a year now.

"Guys, I'm not going to change my mind. I can't revive Negative Impression. I just can't. It was good, but I just can't go back."

Mo snorted. "You idiot. If you'd actually talked to us, you'd know we feel the same."

"Really?"

Luke nodded. "Yes. Mo wants to spend more time with his family. And…." He looked bashful. "Lily's pregnant."

"Congratulations!" Devlin leaned over and gave Luke a half clench.

Mo spoke again. "Touring was already getting hard. Without Trent… well, neither of us have any interest in trying to find out if we can slot in another guitarist like finding the missing piece of a puzzle. We worked together, the four of us. And we'll always be friends. Brothers. But Negative Impression is done."

Devlin heaved out a sigh of relief. Most of his avoidance had been selfish, but part of it had been fear that his inability to revive Negative Impression would be detrimental to Mo and Luke.

"Done," he echoed. Jack threaded their fingers together.

Lily called for Luke to join her in the living room, and Mo followed.

Jack let go of him to pick at the platter of turkey, snagging a few more bites and licking his fingers.

"Was it you or my mother who planned this?" Devlin kept his voice neutral.

A gusty sigh ruffled Jack's hair. "I suggested your mom invite them. You… seemed to have turned a corner, and we both thought you'd regret it if you kept avoiding them."

Devlin looked deep into Jack's piercing blue eyes that had become so dear. "Thank you. You gave me back my music, you helped me remember Trent, and you mended fences I didn't know could be mended. Thank you, so much."

Jack's lip trembled. "I love you. I just wanted what was best for you."

Devlin's mood rocketed up, like he'd been carrying around a heavy weight that had suddenly disappeared. "I love you too." And he knew that this day would always be one of his favorite memories.

KC Burn has been writing for as long as she can remember and is a sucker for happy endings (of all kinds). After moving from Toronto to Florida for her husband to take a dream job, she discovered a love of gay romance and fulfilled a dream of her own—getting published. After a few years of editing web content by day, and neglecting her supportive, understanding hubby and needy cat at night to write stories about men loving men, she was uprooted yet again and now resides in California. Writing is always fun and rewarding, but writing about her guys is the most fun she's had in a long time, and she hopes you'll enjoy them as much as she does.

Website: kcburn.com
Twitter: @authorkcburn
Facebook: www.facebook.com/kcburn

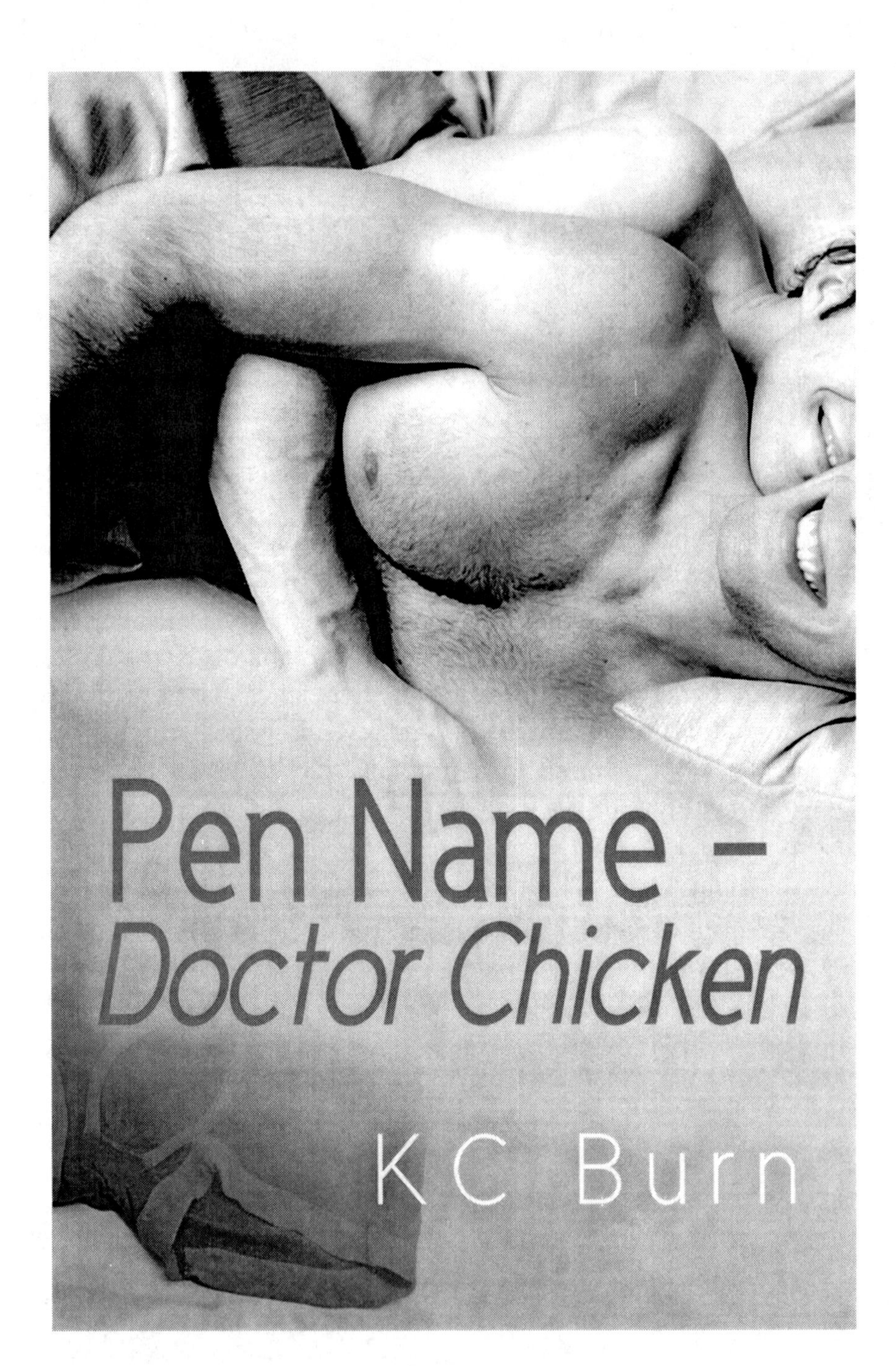
Pen Name –
Doctor Chicken
KC Burn

Sometimes Stratford Dale feels like Doctor Chicken consumes his life. It's his pen name for a series of wildly popular children's books. They were his brainchild; he meant for them to be a way to pay his many bills while he pursued his dream of publishing graphic novels. But the Doctor Chicken contract was a raw deal. Instead, he churns out book after book for a pittance, leaving him broke and no closer to his dreams.

Stratford's dreams of love have fared no better, but he's still trying. After yet another disastrous date, he's intrigued by a man going into a cooking class—so he takes the class too. Vinnie Giani is a successful, self-made man who is charmed by Stratford's bow ties, sharp humor, and clumsiness—which leads to an opportunity to take Stratford in for stitches. Vinnie is, above all, responsible, having taken on the care of his mother and sisters from a young age. Perhaps it's natural when he begins to treat Stratford more as a child who needs a parent than as an equal partner. But when Vinnie tries to "fix" Stratford's career woes—including the Doctor Chicken problem—and ends up making the situation worse, their fledgling relationship may not withstand the the strain created by blame and lies.

www.dreamspinnerpress.com

RAINBOW BLUES

KC Burn

Having come out late in life, forty-three-year-old Luke Jordan is at a loss about how to conduct himself as a gay man. As a construction manager, he's not interested in being out at work, but he'd like to find a boyfriend or at least some gay friends. Two years after his wife got all their friends in the divorce, he's no closer to the life he wants.

Zach, Luke's adult son, takes charge and signs him up for the Rainbow Blues, a social group for gay blue-collar workers. At an event, he not only finds friends but meets Jimmy Alexander, part-time stage actor and full-time high school biology teacher. Jimmy loves the stage but wishes potential boyfriends weren't so jealous of the time he devotes to it. When he meets Luke and finds him accepting of his many facets, he thinks it's a dream come true.

Their relationship quickly moves into serious territory, but their connection is tested to its breaking point by the offer of a juicy movie role that takes Jimmy to the opposite coast and into the path of a very sexy costar.

www.dreamspinnerpress.com

TEA or
CONSEQUENCES
KC Burn

Riley Parker: temp, twink, geek… sleuth?

Maybe Riley isn't living up to his full potential, but being a temp executive assistant suits him. He's never bored at work, he's got friends who let him geek out, and he's got a carefully crafted twink exterior… which might be getting constrictive now that he's on the other side of thirty. Life isn't perfect, but it's comfortable.

It all unravels when he takes a job working for a tea-obsessed cosmetics queen, the owner of Gautier Cosmetics. During the launch party for a new product, Riley finds his boss dead under suspicious circumstances, and the homicide detective is none other than Tadeo Martin, Riley's high school obsession who never knew he was alive.

Tad drafts Riley to get the scoop on the inner workings of Gautier, and for Riley, it's like a drug. His natural inquisitiveness is rewarded with more and more Tad. Unfortunately, his snooping puts him in the running for two other roles: suspect and victim. The killer doesn't care which.

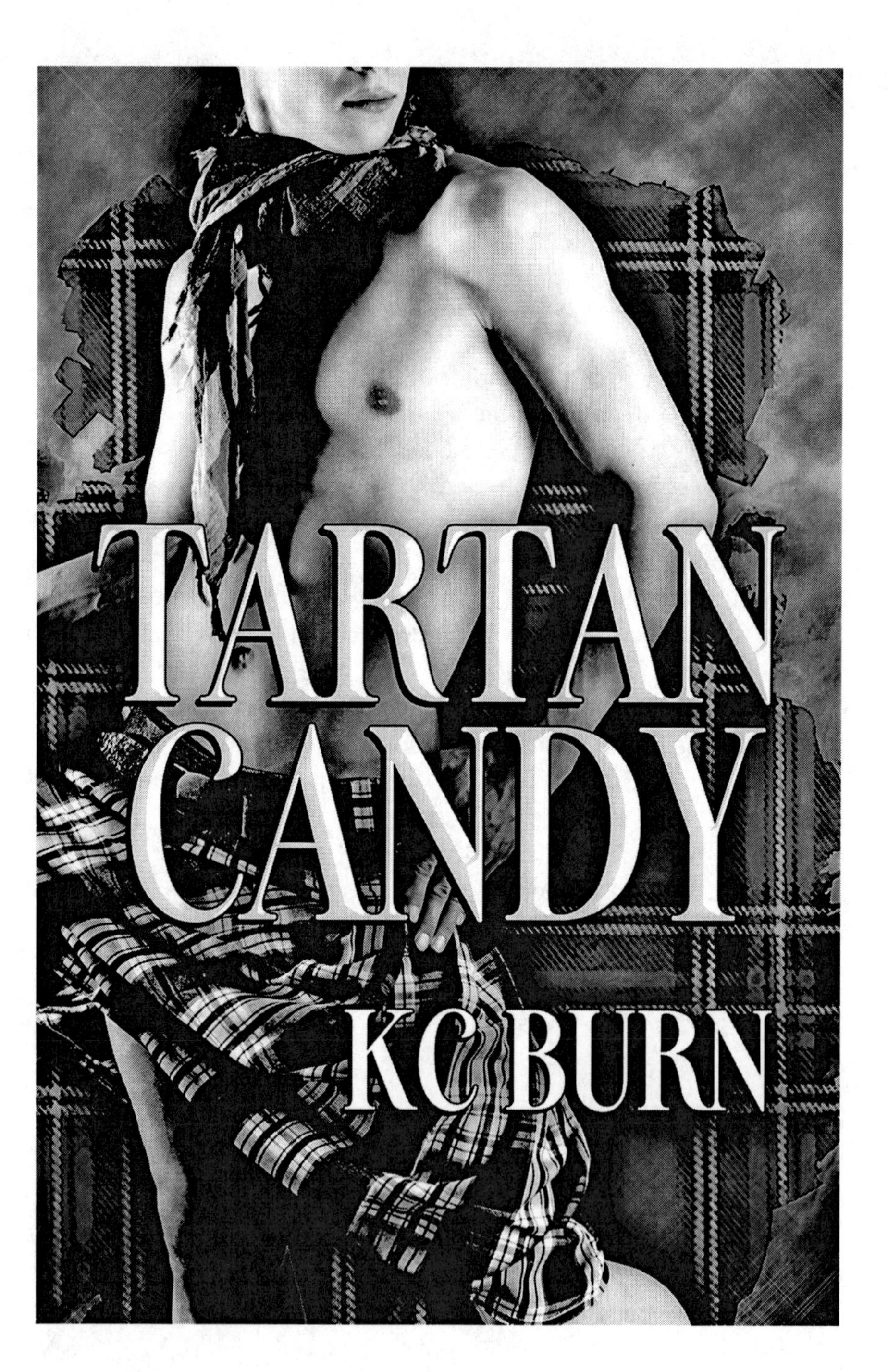
TARTAN
CANDY
KC BURN

A Fabric Hearts Story

Finlay McIntyre (aka Raven) is a successful adult film star with a penchant for kilts, until an accident cuts short his stardom and leaves him with zero sexual desire, lowered self-esteem, and no job. He knew his porn career wouldn't last forever, but he wasn't prepared for retirement at twenty-eight. While trying to figure out the rest of his life, Raven agrees to attend a high school reunion. That's when a malfunctioning AC unit in his hotel room changes everything.

Caleb Sanderson, an entrepreneur with his own HVAC business, has no idea what to expect when he steps into Raven's hotel room to fix his AC unit. They're attracted to each other, but Caleb, closeted, can't afford a gay relationship, not with his mom pressuring him to produce grandchildren. If he wants to keep Raven—who no closet could hold—he'll need to tell his family the truth. But Raven has a few secrets of his own. He refuses to reveal his porn past to Caleb, a past that might be the final obstacle to Caleb and Raven having any kind of relationship.

www.dreamspinnerpress.com

PLAID VERSUS PAISLEY

KC BURN

A Fabric Hearts Story

Two years after his life fell apart, Will Dawson moved to Florida to start over. His job in the tech department of Idyll Fling, a gay porn studio, is ideal for him. When his boss forces him to take on a new hire, the last person he expects is Dallas Greene—the man who cost him his job and his boyfriend back in Connecticut. He doesn't know what's on Dallas's agenda, but he won't be blindsided by a wolf masquerading as a runway model. Not again.

Dallas might have thrown himself on his brother's mercy, but his skills are needed at Idyll Fling. Working with Will is a bonus, since Dallas has never forgotten the man. A good working relationship is only the beginning of what Dallas wants with Will.

But Dallas doesn't realize how deep Will's distrust runs, and Will doesn't know that the man he's torn between loving and hating is the boss's brother. When all truths are revealed, how can a relationship built on lies still stand?

JUST ADD
ARGYLE
KC BURN

A Fabric Hearts Story

Tate Buchanan is a troublemaker who can't keep a job, no matter how many times his lucky argyle sweater gets him hired. Add to that a learning disability and an impetuous nature that sends him into altercations to protect the defenseless, and he hardly manages to make friends, let alone find a man who's interested in him for more than one night.

Most people think EMT Jaime Escobar is a player, but the truth is he wants a serious partner—he just can't justify wasting time on guys he knows aren't a match. But when he treats a gorgeous redhead after a fight, he finds the spark he's spent so many years looking for.

Jaime wants to take the next step with Tate, but it's clear Tate's not going to curb his impulsive behavior—his next fight sends him to the hospital. Jaime's relationship with a near criminal isn't something his family is ready to accept, not any more than Tate is willing to be kept a secret. Jaime will need a lot of understanding—and some luck of his own—to keep them both. But this is one fight he's going to see through to the end.